Book 6

Copyright © 2020 by A.J. Rivers

All rights reserved.

No part of this book may be reproduced in any form or by any electronic or mechanical means, including information storage and retrieval systems, without written permission from the author, except for the use of brief quotations in a book review.

❦ Created with Vellum

# THE GIRL AND THE HUNT

A.J. RIVERS

# CHAPTER ONE

The flash of the cameras is blinding.

Around me, the world moves in slow motion. Voices drift past like they're coming through water. Only the sound of the cameras, the impossibly, unnaturally loud snap of each second being captured, pierces through the fog. Each click of the shutter slices through time, creating moments like slivers of glass.

Somewhere in the back of my mind, I'm aware of someone talking to me. I'm not sure who it is. The voice is muffled by the pressure closing in around me and the sound of the blood rushing in my ears. A touch on my shoulder turns me around, and I stretch my hands out in front of me. The flashes glisten off the blood smeared on my palms and dotted on my fingertips. I turn them over to show the wet streaks of brilliant red across the backs of my hands and up onto my wrists.

They shouldn't be there. I know that as well as any of the people around me. If I'd done what I was supposed to do, reacted the way I was supposed to react, there would be no blood on my skin. But that's like looking over your shoulder in a photograph. No matter what's there, you can't change what's behind you.

I walked into the house before Sam. He was right behind me, close enough to hear me breathe, but not enough to stop me when I ran for the family room. I knew the layout of the house. It was familiar beneath my feet, even though I'd never been in the house. The only time I was here during the last time I was in Feathered Nest was when I stood in the front yard and talked to Marren Purcell while she showed me pictures of her roses. She grew beautiful roses. They crawled on vines up trellises and reach toward the porch, casting shadows on the front of the house and standing out against the white siding in pops of pink and peach. Not now, though. The vines are cold and dry; the early February sunlight not yet warm enough to coax out the leaves and unfurl the buds.

It's just as well. Pink roses look out of place at a grave.

That's what Marren's house will always be now. Even when her tattered body is brought out of the family room and the darkened carpet is replaced. Even when the splatters of blood are washed away, and the words scrawled on the wall are covered with a coat of fresh white paint meant to keep all the house's secrets. After everything is done and time has passed, it will still be a grave.

When I'd visited Marren the first time I was in Feathered Nest, she was so proud to show me the pictures of her roses. Later I saw pictures of the roses in full bloom in a newspaper clipping from years before. She'd won a now-defunct garden contest. I didn't go into the house then, but I know it now. It was easy to navigate when I opened the front door and stepped inside because it was like stepping inside Jake Logan's house. Though his stood several streets away, they were built from the same plans, laid out in the same way. I imagine there are many houses throughout the tiny town just like it.

Sam didn't stop me when I ran through the formal living room at the front of the house. He might have called out to me when I got into the family room set in the center of the house or tried to stop me from reaching down toward Marren's body stretched out across the carpet. If he did, I didn't hear it. My mind wasn't on him. It was on her eyes staring up at the ceiling and the blood pooling beneath her. It was on the note pinned to her chest with my name written across it.

My hands were already on her when he came into the room and told me to stop so they could take pictures. Everything needed to be photographed exactly the way it was when we found her. I didn't plan on moving her. I just wanted the note. It's in an evidence bag now, ready to be brought to the police station and processed along with all the rest of the evidence. That's all the room has been reduced to now. Evidence.

Pictures, swabs, segments of carpet and fabric, objects splattered with blood. The room dismantled and relegated to plastic bags and cardboard boxes as the investigation team compartmentalizes each element of the crime. It feels somehow safer that way. Precise and controlled. But also cold. A life has been reduced to a puzzle.

It doesn't matter that the note was taken from my hands by the first officer to respond. I don't need the paper or the gold safety pin that held it to her chest. Even if the words weren't burned into my mind, I had Sam take a picture of the note when the officers were still on their way. It started in the flowing script of the second half of the note we found with the flowers on the car and on the letter sent with the train ticket that shoved me headlong into horror almost a week ago. Halfway down the note, the handwriting changed, shifting back to the heavy black block letters all too familiar to me.

*You missed the tea party, Emma.*
*It was lovely.*
*Spice tea and cake.*
*The last, but not the first.*
*It's a shame it's still cold.*
*No flowers for the party.*
*But not too much of a loss.*
*I've always thought roses should be read.*
*These remind me of her funeral.*
*Such a simple casket.*
*Is that why it seemed so light?*
*I know.*
*Come find out.*
*Catch me*

The officer stops taking pictures of my hands and steps further into the family room. They've already draped a white sheet over Marren. She's just a piece of the puzzle now. Evidence. They'll slip her into a plastic bag and bring her to a box. Examine her. Pick her over. Try to piece her back together again and hope she can still tell her secrets.

Sam steps up beside me and puts his arm around my waist, pulling me close. I don't know if he's trying to comfort me or make sure I stay on my feet. But it's not really necessary. I'm steady now. I have to be. I watch the officer take more pictures and another start setting down the markers of what they'll take with them when they leave. I know I can't just walk away from this. I can't hand it over to them and let them figure it out. Because they won't. It's not about them.

My mind starts to settle as awareness comes back and everything sharpens again. What felt slow and washed out returns to crystal focus, and I can hear the stomp of heavy footsteps come up the front steps toward the door. My eyes lock on the pool of sunlight stretching across the living room floor just before a foreboding form swallows it.

"Chief, we're processing the scene," says an officer who looks like tired and worn are his perpetual states. "Right now, there doesn't appear to be any sign of forced entry. No murder weapon has been located."

Police Chief LaRoche ignores the officer and takes long strides across the room to me. His eyes hook into me, all signs of the reluctant respect that was there during our brief conversation outside the courthouse the last time I saw him gone.

"Emma Griffin," he says with a slight growl in his voice.

Sam steps up to put himself protectively between LaRoche and me. His face stays calm and steady. It's an expression I recognize from being on investigations with him when he has to contend with those involved while trying to keep tensions under control.

"Sheriff Sam Johnson, Sherwood County," he says, offering his hand.

LaRoche looks at it but doesn't reach for it.

"I know who you are." His stare shifts back to me. "What are you doing here?"

In that second, the emotion locked tight inside me bubbles over. I step past Sam to confront the chief.

"I'm doing what *you* were supposed to do," I shout. "You said you would check on her."

"You called me three hours ago, Griffin," he snaps back.

"And you said you would make sure she was alright. I told you to come here and make sure she was alright, to talk to her, and warn her to stay inside until I got here."

"I came," he tells me.

"When?" I ask. "Did you come as soon as I called you?"

"I'm not at your beck and call. There were other things I was in the middle of handling, and I needed to finish those first before I could come out here. I drove by and noticed her car wasn't here, and her shades were down. It took me some time to get back, but when I did, I knocked on the door, and she didn't answer. She's been out of town, so I figured she hadn't gotten back yet," he says.

"She didn't answer because she was dead!" I shout.

Sam grabs my shoulders and pulls me back away from the police chief.

"Emma," he says. "Calm down."

"I'm not going to calm down. If he did what he was supposed to do, she might still be alive."

"Don't blame me for this," LaRoche warns. "She might have been dead by the time you called me."

I recoil at the cold note in his voice. He draws in a breath as I pull closer to him, my jaw set.

"That woman was lying there in a pool of her own blood, alone."

"Until you found her."

"What's that supposed to mean?" I ask angrily.

"Who did you bring to my town?" he growls.

My heart squeezes tightly in my chest, painfully constricting my breath. The coroner comes into the house, and I step out of the way, turning to look over my shoulder at Marren a final time. Only hours ago, her kind blue eyes looked into the face of evil. A sick feeling rolls through me as I wonder if she watched the words written across the wall in her own blood.

*Where's your mother, Emma?*

## CHAPTER TWO

### IAN

SEVENTEEN YEARS AGO...

He said goodbye. Ian knew he did. Before Mariya left the house, suitcase in hand, he held her close and said goodbye. But that wasn't supposed to be the last time. Those weren't the last of the words he had to say to her. There were so many more.

They were owed so many more years. He could feel them when he walked back into the house. Sweat sticking the thin fabric of his shirt to his skin, the spring night outside still humid, he walked into a silent world of unfulfilled promises. With every step, he encountered something that should have happened but never had the opportunity to. The rooms around him echoed with breaths never taken, laughs that never happened. Whispers that would never be heard. Out of the corners of his eyes he almost caught movement, like he was watching the ghosts of moments meant to unfold that were stolen from reality.

He felt those words in his mouth. They rolled on his tongue and swelled in his throat. They ached in his chest and churned in his stomach. All those words were things he was meant to say, but he would never be able to now. Even if he did, he would only be saying them into the void. There was no one there to hear them now. No one to scoop them up out of the air and replace them with her own. That goodbye he said when she walked out of the house and to the waiting car wasn't meant to be the final one. It fulfilled a role it could never live up to. That goodbye was only meant as a bridge, only meant to last a few days. Now it had to stretch, to hang on for the rest of his life.

How many more goodbyes were meant to be spoken between them? How many I love you's existed in the corners of his mind and waiting in his mouth? What else was there? What other words did he not even know he was going to say to her?

He felt the phantom words there in the silence. They pressed in around him now that the teams that swarmed the house were gone. It had all happened so fast he barely even had a chance to process what was going on, and now it was over, and reality crashed in around him.

Ian didn't remember making any phone calls. Obviously, he had, or the people wouldn't have come. But he couldn't remember picking up the phone or dialing. He didn't know who he called first or what he said. All he knew was that, in what seemed like an instant, the house went from calm and full of promise to bursting with voices and people. He tried to keep up with them, to listen to what they were saying to him, and tell them the things they needed to know. But he didn't know. They were asking questions he had no answers to. Questions he wanted to ask them.

He thought he'd held her. He wanted to hold her in his arms as soon as he saw her lying there on the floor, but now, hours later, he looked down at himself and realized there was no blood. He didn't understand. As soon as he heard the unmistakable slicing sound of the silenced bullet and the impact of a body against the floor, his memories stopped. He couldn't remember anything until the stretcher slid by with the white sheet covering her. He couldn't see her face. He didn't know if her eyes were open or closed, or where the bullet went in. As soon as that realization sunk in, he clawed through his mind, ripping it apart in search of even a flicker from when he found her.

But there was nothing. Those moments weren't there. They'd been wiped from his mind, blocked from his memory. His brain did it to protect him, but it was torture. Why didn't he touch her?

Seeing them bring her out of the house was the last thing he could concretely remember for the next several hours. There were pieces of memories, shards, and fragments he could start to piece together. He knew he was brought in to answer questions. But he couldn't remember any of the faces or the names of the people who asked them. He didn't know what today was, or when asked, how he responded. Their words sank into him and dragged out responses. There was nothing voluntary. Not that he was trying to hide anything. There was nothing to hide. He would tell them anything, offer whatever was in him to give. He would willingly carve his heart out, peel away every layer of his mind, anything that would give them what they wanted to know.

There was only one face he clearly remembered. One face staring at him through the roiling sea of people that flooded the house and spilled out in the lawn, dripping into the road blocked with chasing lights. There was no sound. No sirens. But there was that face. Ian met his eyes for half a second, only long enough to know he was there. The man should have been there before. It was only minutes, but they slipped away and took Mariya with them. Those minutes turned her from what was into what used to be. Reduced her to sand at the bottom of an hourglass.

Ian didn't think again for a long time. Not until after the questions. After the long ride home. After walking back through the door. That's when it brought him to the floor. He sat against the door, trying to breathe, but there was no air. He was existing outside of reality; in borrowed space that overlapped the world, he'd lived in only hours before. It wasn't until he felt her sit down beside him that he started to inhabit the world again. His daughter sitting there beside him pulled him back and made him feel real again.

He didn't say anything to her. He couldn't. Emma didn't ask. She sat there, close enough to lean her head against his shoulder, and breathed. Those were his breaths now. They would fill his lungs and push back out into the empty, hollow rooms. They would force his heart to keep beating, stop the blood from drying in his veins. Eyes just like his, but a face like her mother's. She would keep him there.

They sat there as the last of the night faded, and the darkness cast through the windows above the door became less saturated. Ian didn't want the sun to rise. He willed the horizon to hold on, to cling to the night just a little longer. Once it broke open and allowed the light to come, he knew it would really be over. The time ticking by on the grandfather clock in the corner of the foyer didn't matter. It was the night that kept him close to Mariya. As long as it was dark, they were still together in that night. He could still share that space with her.

When the light came, it would all be gone. With the first sliver of rose gold glowed against the dark edge of the sky, they would be irreparably separated. He would move forward into the first day without her on this planet with him, and she would stay forever in that last night.

But the sun came, as he knew it would. It broke through the windows above the door and filtered onto the foyer floor in front of them. Ian couldn't resist it any longer. He got up and scooped Emma into his arms to carry her into the living room. He laid her onto the couch and pulled a blanket down over her. It came down from the back of the couch carrying the scent of her mother, the one who last used it.

He could have brought his daughter upstairs into her room to sleep, but he didn't want to go to the upper floor of the house. He didn't want to walk past his bedroom and see Mariya's shoes on the floor or the closet door standing slightly open like she always left it. Someone else would do that for him. Right now, there were other things he had to do. He would let Emma rest. As long as she was sleeping, he didn't have to worry about her so much. He could get the arrangements in place while she was protected by the quiet in her mind.

Ian walked into the kitchen and picked up the phone. There were a few numbers he knew without having to check his address book, and this was one of them.

"We need to move," he said when the voice came through the other line. "As soon as possible. Make sure the house in Vermont is ready."

"And Mariya?"

He filled his lungs to combat the pain of his heart ripping.

"They still have her. You know their wishes when they release her body," he said, trying to keep the emotion out of his voice.

"Is that it?"

"No," Ian said. "Get in touch with the funeral home and schedule a memorial. Order a casket and flowers. Tell them to contact Spice."

## CHAPTER THREE

NOW

There's never a good way to take a body away from a crime scene. I've witnessed it enough times to have seen every emotion, every thought process, every approach teams take. None of them are right. There are those who are tenuous and delicate about the way they touch the body like they are afraid to offend the person who once occupied that corpse. There are those who seem almost afraid of it, or disgusted. They take too much time, far too overcautious about the way they move the body and transfer it onto the stretcher or into the body bag. Sometimes they approach the task so gingerly they end up dropping the body or making more of a production out of the situation than they need to.

Then there are those who treat the body almost with a level of disdain. Like they want to distance themselves from the thought it was ever a human. These are the ones who scoop the body up like it's nothing and shove it into place without any evidence of respect.

Both make me uncomfortable. I've learned to disconnect myself from the harshest of emotions when it comes to human bodies. In most situations, I'm able to close myself off and see the body as simply another part of the crime scene. Like with the man who tumbled out of the juncture between the two train cars and sent me spiraling into the madness of that trip. I couldn't think about him as a man in those first moments or even the hours that followed.

It would break me to see him as a life, to think of what he might have been doing when he got on the train that day. He couldn't be someone's son, someone's brother, someone's husband, someone's father. If he was any of that, I would have had to think about the blood that soaked his shirt and pooled on the floor as more than just blood. I would have had to think about who else shared that blood, where it came from, the potential it still had. I would have to think about his eyes and wonder what the last thing they saw was, and the voice I'd never heard and wonder what was the last thing it said.

Keeping all that out of my mind meant being able to pull back from the person and think instead about the larger picture. But I didn't see them take him from the train. That is the moment that changes everything, without fail. Zipping the body into a bag or covering it with a sheet on a stretcher is an altering moment. Concealing the body makes it real again, forces it back into the cold starkness of being the tragic remains of a human life.

That's what I'm watching now. The coroner's team lifts Marren's body onto the stretcher and covers her face before pulling her out of the house to load her into the car. I watch until she disappears, my eyes sliding back down to the blood on my hands.

"You need to get out of the way so my team can do their investigation," LaRoche says.

My eyes snap over and I stare at him, blinking a few times and waiting for him to rewind and say something else.

"You can't be serious," I tell him.

"I'm very serious, Griffin. I'm not going to talk about the fact that you showed up here and broke into a woman's house. Right now, I just need you to get out of the way so we can do our jobs and find out who did this."

"You can't honestly think I'm just going to leave?" I sputter.

"And you can't honestly think I will accept anything else," he snaps back. "This isn't your scene, Griffin. You're not undercover. You're not in my department. You are a civilian, and you're a distraction. You've already compromised the scene by touching the body and moving that note. You know better than that."

"Don't you dare scold me," I warn. "Now is not the time for you to start waving your..." I draw in a breath, forcing myself to calm down, "badge around because you want to be in charge of everything."

"I *am* in charge of everything. This is my jurisdiction and my investigation. From what I hear, you aren't an active agent anymore, and unless you're in Sherwood, your deputization means nothing."

"Who are you talking to about my status as an agent?" I ask.

"That's not relevant to the conversation," he tells me.

"Whoever it is has been misinformed. I've spoken to Creagan about adjusting and redefining my role within the Bureau. I haven't given up my badge, and I have no intention to."

"Just like a baby with her bottle full of water," LaRoche remarks with a sneer.

"Excuse me?" I ask.

"You've been on leave for how long now?"

"What does my leave have to do with anything?" I ask.

"How many times has Creagan asked when you're coming back to headquarters? When has he asked you to put an end date on your leave?"

"That's between the Bureau and me," I snap. "He knows when I'm ready to be back full-time, I'll let him know. And until then, if he needs my help in an investigation, I'm available. That's the agreement we've always had."

"And yet you still don't have your gun. Your badge is a pacifier, Griffin. It's to keep you feeling like your relevant when they've moved past you. You're a loose cannon. They know if they oust you, you could explode. So, they keep you quiet by reassuring you, by making sure you think you're still a part of it all," he sneers. "You keep your mouth shut, they don't have to deal with the disaster you'll cause. But I have no reason to placate you. The last time you were here, you ripped my town apart. Now you've dragged us into your shit again. I'm not dealing with it."

I glare at LaRoche, all the anger and irritation from the first time I encountered him rushing back. From the first moment I saw him, I didn't trust him. He's slimy and arrogant, misogynistic, and intensely invested in his image. Right now, none of that means anything. This isn't about show or getting attention.

"During my leave, I have assisted the Bureau in three investigations. My current case will require more extensive FBI involvement. This game isn't about you, LaRoche. You can pack your ball and go home. I'm here because I need to be here. And you may have forgotten, but the last time I was in your town, ripping it apart meant catching a killer you couldn't," I tell him, my voice low as I try to maintain some control of myself.

"How about the dead man on your porch?" LaRoche asks. My shoulders square, and my throat tightens as I stare at him silently. "Exactly. Don't believe for a second I don't think that man was here because of you."

Another officer walks between us and into the living room to collect more evidence. They're going to start dismantling the crime scene without me even getting a chance to look around. I have to stop them. As much as it makes me sick to even consider it, I have to feed into him. It's the only way to make him stand down and get out of his defensive mode enough to give me access to the investigation. Without that, I will be at the mercy of what he's willing to release to the public, and that's never going to give me what I need. Not only because he would leave out critical details they find, but because he would miss details he didn't notice or even know to look for. Even ones I don't know to look for.

But I have to be careful about how I do it. This isn't the time to give away more than he already knows.

"Yes. He likely was. And that is linked directly to this. Just as everything that happened on the train is. As soon as I got that note supposedly from Marren Purcell, I knew something was going on, and that's why I wanted you to check on her that day and then again earlier today. I admit all this has to do with me. This is happening because of me. But we don't know why, and that's why I need you to let me be involved. I'm already helping the department actively investigating the murders on the train. The cases are linked, and I could be a liaison between the two of you. If I can answer even one question that might make something make more sense, that would be worth it, right?" I ask.

Just talking to him like this feels sour in my mouth, but I have to keep myself under control. If I can play into his perception of himself, I can convince him to give me the access I need.

"Why would you think I need your help?" he asks.

"Because you do," I insist firmly, some of the softness I've forced into my voice disappearing. "Look at that wall. Whose name is on it?"

"Yours," he admits, never looking at the bloody message.

"Just like on the note pinned to Marren. Just like the notes on the train. This person is doing this because of me. Like I said, this is a game. A sick, twisted, screwed-up, patented by Hades himself game, but a game. And he doesn't want to play with you. He wants to play with me." I draw in a breath. "So let me play."

## CHAPTER FOUR

"He's going to let you shadow the investigation," Sam points out. "Isn't that what you wanted?"

"No," I sigh. "What I wanted was to be a part of the investigation. Not to shadow it. Not to be able to walk around and listen to what people say and let them screw things up without being able to say anything about it. They have no idea what they're dealing with."

"We both know that, but this is what you have to work with right now. You're not going to be able to convince LaRoche to hand over the reins of the investigation. Unfortunately, you're stuck. Unless all the stars align, and LaRoche decides to call in the Bureau within the next few hours, they agree to investigate everything as one case and let you act as an investigating agent; this is all you have. You need to take the opportunity where you have it," he tells me.

"Don't put that too much into the universe," I say.

"What do you mean?" he asks.

"The Bureau might end up involved, especially the more complicated this gets. But if Creagan gets involved, he might make me a consultant rather than letting me actually participate in the investigation itself. That would keep me out of it just as much as LaRoche is, maybe even more. If by some slim miracle he does make me an investigating agent, I'd be locked down. I'd have to follow absolute protocol. Even if it meant not following my instincts. There was a time when I might have been willing to do that, but not when it comes to this," I point out.

"Because you've proven yourself so good at doing that in the last year," Sam teases. "You've stuck stringently to the rules in all the cases I've worked with you."

I roll my eyes and flip the sun visor up.

"I've done what needed to be done. And I've stuck far closer to protocol than a lot of agents and officers I've known would have in the same situations. Sometimes the rules don't fit, and you have to go with your gut and be willing to live with the consequences. I've been facing consequences I'm not willing to live with. And right now, I'm dealing with the same thing. You know as well as I do this isn't just going to go away. Whoever this is has a plan, and they're going to keep going until they've checked off everything on their list. Which means unless I can dig as deep as I need to, it's just going to get worse."

"You can't think that way," Sam says.

"I have to think that way. Do you seriously think this guy is going to have been so sloppy he'd leave clues LaRoche would understand? This isn't some break-in that went bad. It's not a random murder. Marren was chosen. He picked her for a specific reason, and he planned every bit of her death. It might not have gone exactly like he thought it would because I didn't end up here in Feathered Nest a few days ago, but it wasn't just thrown together. The mighty chief isn't going to find dots to connect that are going to create a picture for him. I have to figure it out, and if shadowing is all he'll let me do for his portion of the investigation, then I'm going to have to make the most of that and do the rest on my own," I say.

"Not on your own," Sam tells me, reaching across the car and squeezing my hand. "I'm here, and I'll do whatever I can. You're right. No one understands this the way you do. And that's the point. But I have two more days until I have to be back in Sherwood, and I will give you every minute of those days."

I squeeze his hand back, leaning my head against the seat to look at him.

"Thank you."

The long, narrow road we've been following ends, and Sam lets out a breath, his eyes locked through the windshield on the cabin hunkering in front of us. Cabin 13.

"You're sure about this?" he asks.

I nod, releasing my seatbelt and climbing out of the car. It's been a year since I've stood here, but in so many ways it feels like I'm right back in that moment. But this time I'm not afraid. I refuse to be.

"Yes," I tell him.

"You know he's doing this to mess with your head, right?" Sam asks.

I glance over the top of the car at him.

"Yes."

"And you're still going to stay here?"

"Yes."

"Is this what we've gotten to? You're only going to give me one-word answers from now on?" he asks.

"Yes."

I walk around to the back of the car to get my suitcase from the trunk.

"But you're right. This," I swirl my hand around in a gesture toward the cabin, "is screwed up. I know it. LaRoche knows it. But that's the point. He's trying to throw me off. His little mea culpa at the courthouse always felt like a bunch of bull to me. He only admires me and my work if I'm far away from Feathered Nest. I intimidate him, but more than that, I piss him off. He despises that it took an undercover Bureau agent to solve the serial murders and disappearances here. The last thing he wants is to have the town think he's letting the same thing happen again with another killer. They'll lose trust in him and think he can't keep them safe. But he thinks if he distracts me enough, no one will blame him for the murder and won't think he needs an agent to save his ass again."

"But he does," Sam says.

"Even more than before. Not that I care about saving him. I want to save whoever's next. Maybe myself. And if that takes staying here again, so be it. The closest hotel is outside of town, and I don't want to be that far from everything that's happening. Besides, maybe being here will give me some clarity and help me find the answers I need," I explain.

"What answers are you going to get by being in this cabin again?" Sam asks. "You already solved those murders. Jake Logan is sitting in prison right now because of it. What other answers could you need from here?"

"Ron Murdock," I say simply.

I start for the door and Sam follows me.

"Emma, you don't even know who he was."

"I know he knew my parents. I know someone keeps leading me back to him. And I know somehow or another, his death has something to do with all this. It started with him. Maybe it ends with him, too."

I step up onto the porch with a chill on my skin. The weather is still cool, but it's not as cold now in the early part of February as it was last January when I stepped onto this porch for the first time. Pausing at the top step, I reach out and rest my hand on one of the rough-hewn support beams holding up the roof of the porch. Sam steps up behind me and rests his hand on my back.

"Are you okay?" he asks.

I glance up at him, then at the door to the cabin.

"It almost feels like I'm visiting a movie set. Does that make sense? It's like I wasn't really here, but I watched it happen over and over in my mind, so I know everything about it. My head was in such a different place the first time I was here," I say, looking back at him. "You know?"

Sam shakes his head. "No. You've never really talked to me about it. I know what was in the news and what you found. You told me about Jake and his grandmother. I know about the thimble you took and the flack you got from some people for not falling in line and doing what they thought an agent should do. But you haven't talked much about what happened before that. I didn't ask because I figured you didn't want to talk about it."

I nod, letting out a slow breath.

"Do you want to know?"

"You don't have to talk about it."

"Do you want to know, Sam?"

"Yes."

## CHAPTER FIVE

"You know how Greg and I met. I don't think I need to get into many of the details about that. It's not really applicable to the rest of the story. Suffice it to say things were fine between us. I never really expected to have anything more than 'just fine'. Not after you. When I made the decision to go to training and become an FBI agent, that defined the rest of my life for me. I thought I was structuring my entire future when I made that choice, including any future relationships."

I let out a mirthless laugh and shake my head. "As soon as I walked away from you, I knew that part of my life was never going to be the same. It wasn't that I was going to go have my career and find someone else, and we were going to live happily ever after. I was going to go have my career and settle. If I ever decided to find someone at all."

"Why did you?" Sam asks.

"What do you mean?" I ask. "Why did I what?"

"Why did you have a relationship with Greg? You haven't told me much about him, but from what I do know, he doesn't seem like anyone you would have ever been interested in."

"He wasn't anyone the version of me you knew would be interested in," I clarify. "And that was the point. It had been years, but I was still convinced I could change. The person I was didn't have to be set in stone. I could decide who I was going to be, who I needed to be, and that meant creating the environment that person would live in. Does that make sense?"

"No," Sam says. "Why were you fighting so hard? What was the point of completely altering who you were? I understand you wanted to go into the Bureau, and I didn't agree with it, but what else?"

"Going into the Bureau wasn't something I ever thought about, and yet when I made the decision that it was what I wanted to do, it felt like it was always laid out for me. My father insisted I train in martial arts. He talked to me about current events and laws. It was something I was prepared for from the time I was a young child; I just didn't realize it. Then after he disappeared, it fell into place. But I never wanted to be in the CIA. That's what's strange. You would think if going into service was about avenging my father, I'd literally follow in his footsteps, I'd take up the role he left behind. But I couldn't. That didn't feel right to me."

"Because you couldn't bring yourself to think he was actually gone, that he'd left that role vacant," Sam muses.

I nod. "Even when everybody was giving me their condolences and talking about him like he was dead, I never believed it. That just wouldn't sink in. He was missing. He still is missing. And if he was just missing, then I didn't need to pick up his legacy and carry on. But I needed to do something. Living without my mother and not even knowing what happened to her was something that defined my life. It was a part of me from the time I was twelve years old. I never accepted it. And I never wanted anyone else to go through that. More than that, though, I never wanted another criminal to get away with what they did. That thought was something I couldn't cope with. Someone out there knew what happened to my mother. They killed her and were going about their lives like it never happened.

"Every time I thought about that, it just made me angrier. It was like every day they were alive took her life more. Like every day they were alive, it killed her again. I wanted to make sure that didn't happen. Becoming an agent was a way to stop it. But in my heart, I knew that wasn't the life I had planned. I was going to have to sacrifice who I used to be and who I could have been in order to fill that role. The woman I needed to be would have been interested in Greg. On paper, he was everything I should have wanted. Intelligent, successful, in the same industry, so he understood my career pressures and what I was going through."

"So, you played matchmaker with Greg and the person you were telling yourself you had to be," Sam notes.

"You could put it that way. It didn't even really bother me that I wasn't happy with him. It's not that I was unhappy. There weren't real struggles in our relationship. We didn't argue or make each other angry. Pretty much as soon as we started dating, we fell into a really easy pattern that felt like we could've kept it going on into perpetuity. And to be honest, that was pretty much the plan. It wasn't that being in a relationship with him fulfilled me, but it took a layer of pressure off. People expected me to have a relationship and get married. Attaching to Greg, I meant I didn't have to think about that anymore. I didn't have to deal with the idea of meeting people and getting to know them. I didn't want to let anyone in. I didn't want to share my past or wait for that inevitable moment when they would realize who I was and what I've been through and run."

"Did Greg know your past?" Sam asks.

"Some of it," I tell him. "It's hard not to know my mother was murdered or that I've been on my own since I was eighteen. And with as many connections with the Bureau as my father had, his name is known. But I never felt the need to fully open up to him. Not in a way that felt vulnerable, or like I was giving him any more access than newspapers and other people could give him. That was comfortable for me. He was just another piece of building the person and the future I thought I needed. I told myself that if I just kept going, kept reminding myself of that person; I would really become her."

"But you're not."

"That's the thing, Sam. I am. Being an agent might not be what I thought I was going to be. It's not the future I envisioned. But it's what

I am. Who I am. It gives me what I wanted it to, and now it's leading me down the path that brought me to it in the first place. Bit by bit, I'm finding out what happened to my mother."

He looks hurt, and I reach out for his hand before he can step away from me. "But that doesn't mean I was completely right. I didn't have to change everything about myself in order to be a good agent. I just didn't know that before Greg disappeared."

"Did you really see a future with him?" he asks.

"As much as I really let myself see any future," I tell him. "It wasn't really something I thought about very much. I focused on the day to day, and that was it. But as far as our relationship went, I thought everything was going well. Like I said, we didn't argue or aggravate each other. We had a pretty consistent rhythm to our relationship and it just flowed right along. The ring he gave me wasn't an engagement ring. I was clear on that. But I also knew it meant he was thinking in that direction. Then it just ended. There was no build up, no tension in our relationship. No argument, no difficulties that might give me some sort of clue he was thinking about breaking up with me."

"How did he do it?" Sam asks.

"He walked into my office like he did every day. But instead of asking if we were going to dinner or going to order something, he told me he'd been thinking about his life and had come to the conclusion that he needed to go in another direction. That's actually how he put it. Not that he wanted to see other people, or that we weren't working out. Just that he needed to go in another direction."

"You didn't ask him what was going on or try to get some other explanation?"

"I didn't. Looking back on it, that probably says more than anything else. But I just let him walk out of the office. And I was sad. Genuinely, I was. Even if there were no violins and butterflies when it came to our relationship, it was still a relationship I'd had for a long time. Bellamy did everything she could to make me stop thinking about him and convince me it was better that we were broken up. He was boring and had pretty much peaked in his life. She didn't realize I didn't need her to convince me there was more out there than Greg. I just needed to deal with the change and move on. But I didn't get a chance to. Three weeks later, he was gone."

"Just like that?" Sam asks. "He was just gone?"

"Just like that," I nod. "And the first thing I thought was I should have asked him more."

## CHAPTER SIX

### GREG

TWO YEARS AGO...

The self-checkout machine whirred and clicked its way through counting out the hundred dollars Greg requested, then dispensed the bills. He grabbed them from the slot at the front of the machine, folded them in half, and tucked them away in his pocket. Taking the few bags of items he purchased from the frame supporting the bags, he headed out of the store without making eye contact with anybody else. It was a process he had gone through several times over the course of the last three weeks. Combined with shifting money into new accounts and paying bills that didn't exist just so he could access the funds without it being traceable.

He didn't want anybody to be able to look at his bank account in the coming days and weeks and follow his movements. This had to be done carefully. It was one of the steps in the preparation Lotan warned him about during their first encounter in the parking deck. He'd gone into more detail during their second meeting the next day, instructing Greg about everything he needed to do in order to get ready for the mission ahead. For the last nearly three weeks, he had been carefully following each of the guidelines the older man gave him. Greg still didn't know exactly what he was doing or what to expect. Lotan said it was too sensitive to talk about until the time was right.

It still felt so strange to force himself to think of him using that name. It wasn't the first time he was instructed to use a code term to refer to someone on a team, especially when preparing for an undercover assignment that could be dangerous. Using codenames doesn't just help to protect the identity of the people on the team and establish a sense of structure among the ranks. It also creates a certain sense of distance. That seems like a strange thing to want when you're relying on others and working so intently together, but it could be critical to not only the success of the mission but the safety of everyone working together. It's difficult to continue to refer to somebody by their given name while trying to see them as a different person. Giving them a new name or a title creates that distance, helps to blur the person they used to be, so it becomes easier to adapt to them fulfilling another role.

As much as he didn't want to think about it, he also knew it helps to provide a buffer in the event something goes wrong on the assignment. That isn't something any agent ever wants to think about. But it happens. Far more often than he wanted to admit, far more often than is acceptable. Of course, no loss of one of their own is ever acceptable. But when it does happen, the entire assignment becomes at risk. If the rest of the team allow the casualty to affect them too deeply, they only place themselves in more danger. Using a different name creates enough separation to lessen the blow. Operatives could contain the reaction, hold it back until the job was done, then allow themselves to experience their genuine reaction.

But that process always involves the Bureau. Operations with men and women Greg had worked with before. It was harder to get himself accustomed to using a cover name for someone he never met, someone he thought was dead.

Even though he knew who he was dealing with, Greg couldn't say the name Ian Griffin. Emma's father. He couldn't talk about the man's disappearance years before. Over the last three weeks, he'd been given only a few sparse details to fill in his questions about where he'd disappeared to, and why he'd been gone for so long. It was just enough for him to know this man wasn't who everyone thought he was. And that was exactly his intention.

Though he was admired and respected as a top agent in the CIA, Greg learned Ian—Lotan—had another life, another career he had to keep hidden from others. He was also a special operative deputized by the FBI, responsible for top-top-secret operations only possible through the slight hint of overlapping jurisdictions the two organizations had. He worked simultaneously with both organizations to uncover large scale criminal conspiracies and put protective measures into place to manage and reduce the risk to public safety. It wasn't something Greg was even aware was happening, but that was the intentions of both agencies. Ian was one of a very select few individuals who held these massive responsibilities in their hands. And because of that, he was forced to shed his past, his life, and his name.

He became Lotan, and he worked diligently for years before he came looking for Greg.

This was the most intense thing ever asked of Greg. When he committed himself to the Bureau, he knew he might be put into difficult situations. He could be asked to sacrifice his safety, and more, for the cases he would help investigate. But he never anticipated something quite like this. Lotan came to him, asking for his help with something bigger and more important than he ever imagined. It would give him the opportunity to save countless lives and protect not only the nation but nations across the world. It was an honor and a privilege.

In exchange, he was being asked to offer up everything he held dear in his life. He would have to prove his devotion to the Bureau and to the oath he took when he became an agent. Wanting to do his part and make this vision a reality meant being willing to forgo everything. His daily routine. His home. His friends. Emma.

Ending his relationship with Emma was painful, but he reassured himself, it didn't have to be permanent. It was only for as long as he was on this assignment, and it was essential. Maintaining a relationship with her would create more worry, would link him back to his current life, and stop him from being truly able to commit everything to the work he would do with Lotan. Their relationship was going so well. He was happy with her and saw her as his future. But that only made it more important to distance himself from her. He had to protect her. To keep her safe and to ease her reaction. If they were still together when the time finally came for him to walk away, it would be more difficult for her, and she would be more likely to dedicate her time and energy to trying to find him. If their relationship was over, she might be able to just let it go.

At least for now. At least until he was able to come back and explain everything to her. Greg looked forward to that day. This is what he needed to be doing, it was the right choice, and he took solace in knowing the person asking him to do it understood the sacrifice better than anyone. The man once known as Ian put everything behind him, including Emma. It was different, of course, but it was enough.

He only wished he better understood Emma's reaction. She barely gave a response when he told her their relationship was over. It was almost as if she didn't hear it or didn't understand what he was saying. But he couldn't double back. He couldn't stop and talk to her about it. If he did, it would threaten his resolve. Instead, he walked away from her and spent the last three weeks avoiding any contact so they would never have to have that conversation.

It got harder every day, and even as the anxiety about what was to come increased, it was a relief to get to now. It was finally over. This was the last night before he walked away.

Before he disappeared.

Greg got to the borrowed car delivered to his home that afternoon and put everything in the backseat. What was already there didn't look like enough to represent his entire life. But it was all he was able to bring. Too much would call attention. The point was to slip out of his life as if he was never there. He couldn't leave a trail or show that walking away was planned. They would trace his movements, and that wasn't something he could let happen. Of course, they would try.

That was simply the reaction when someone went missing. Especially an agent. When the rest of the team noticed he wasn't following his usual routine and didn't show up for work, they would follow the procedure for trying to find him.

Check his home.

Search for his car.

Follow the money.

The last three weeks were spent ensuring all those details were managed so they would find nothing to lead them to what he was really doing and compromise the assignment. There would be no signs of him planning to leave his life. No signs of foul play. It would look like he simply faded away. And that's exactly what he wanted.

# CHAPTER SEVEN

NOW

"I felt so guilty after he disappeared," I tell Sam. "That's the thing people don't understand about it. They saw me trying to piece it together and figure out what happened because it only made sense I would be devastated by him being gone. Most of the people we knew thought our breakup was really sudden, and a lot just figured we would end up back together. Seeing us together was reassuring to them in some way. That sounds ridiculous now, but it was. In those days and weeks and months after Greg walked out of work and never came back, it was just expected I was going to be sad because my heart was broken, and I was so worried about him. But that's not what was happening."

"You weren't worried?" he asks.

"Of course I was worried. But I wasn't heartbroken. I was upset, sure. I was scared. I didn't want anything to happen to him, but there was never a moment when I really felt crushed by him being gone. What I was going through was guilt."

"Guilt about what?"

"That I didn't do anything else. That I pushed him away or didn't listen to him well enough so I could remember something he said that might tell us where he was. That I didn't ask more questions when he broke up with me or try to figure out what was going through his mind. That it was so easy for me to transition into life without him," I tell him.

"None of that was malicious. You can't blame yourself for things you had no way of knowing were going to matter. People end relationships every single day. That doesn't mean one of the people is going to end up disappearing in a few weeks. You couldn't have known anything was going to happen," Sam tries to reassure me.

"But I should have. One thing anybody who knew Greg would point out about him is his predictability. Routines and schedules. Patterns. Everything just so. That's actually one of the last arguments we had. I was a few minutes late leaving work, so we weren't going to get to the restaurant we ate at every Friday at the same time. He was so upset. It was like he thought the entire world was going to collapse around him because he wasn't sitting in the exact right chair, at the exact right time. That's why I should have thought about the breakup more. It didn't make sense, and it didn't sound like him. It should have tipped me off. If he was going to break up with me, he would have presented all the reasons why in a chart and provided evidence and research to support each of his points, then scheduled a check-in meeting to make sure things were still going well and we were adjusting properly after. That's just the way Greg was," I say.

"Is."

I turn away from the shadows lengthening across the porch and spilling down onto the ground in front of the cabin.

"What?" I ask.

"*Is*. That's the way Greg is. You said 'was'. He's alive, Emma," Sam points out.

I let out a short, mirthless laugh and nod.

"You know, in therapy, Katherine pointed out I never speak about my father in the past tense unless I'm talking about a specific memory from years ago. It's not that he was warm and loving, or that he was one of the best the CIA had to offer. Always that he *is*. I did the same for Greg. I defended the idea of him being alive every time I spoke to her about him. She wanted me to come to terms with it, but I never thought there was something to come to terms with. He was missing, that's it. Now I find out he's alive and suddenly, I've put him in the past. What does that say about me?" I ask.

"Emma, I need to ask you something," he says gingerly. "The picture that was with Greg when they found him..."

I already know what it is, and I don't want to hear it. I'm not there yet, not ready to make sense of any of it. So I keep going.

"It's hard to explain how much his disappearance got to me. There was this sense of 'it's happening again'. First my mother. Then my father. Then Greg. Him going missing made everything so fresh again. I was experiencing that pain all over again because it never went away. It never could," I say.

"Emma..."

"No one was able to explain what happened to either of them, so there was no real way for me to get through the thoughts and feelings and put them behind me. My mother was dead. Is dead. There's no ambiguity in that, but it's not knowing how or why that's made it so I can't process those feelings completely and move on. They got tucked away into the back corner of my mind, and I moved forward. Then when my father disappeared, there was again no explanation. No good reason. Nothing for me to grasp onto so I could at least try to cope with it. After a while, I forced those feelings into the back of my mind too. It wasn't that I couldn't feel it anymore, or that I didn't think about it. I just needed to not have those thoughts front and center all the time, or I wouldn't be able to function."

"Emma, I know you said the scars don't match, but..."

"Then there was Greg. Again, somebody in my life was gone, and I had no idea why. This time, it was all around me. My father protected me when my mother died. I dealt with my father's disappearance by myself except for the very small circle I talked to about it. Everything was controlled. With Greg, I didn't have that chance. I was bombarded with images of him. News stories. People asking me questions and prying way too deep to try to figure it out, while other people put up blocks to prevent me from having anything to do with it. And just like that, I cracked. A few months after he disappeared, it all got to me. A stupid remark pushed me over the edge, and I completely bungled that undercover assignment. It got me six months of desk duty and funneled me right here to Feathered Nest."

"Emma," Sam says, slightly more firmly this time.

My head snaps in his direction.

"I don't know who he is, Sam. The man in that picture isn't my father, and the only explanation is he's his brother. That fits with his appearance and with the birth record from Iowa. But I never knew about my father having a brother, much less a twin. It sounds like a soap opera; only I'm fairly certain nobody is going to be returning from the dead any time soon."

"You had no idea you have an uncle?"

"None. I never met him or heard of him. My entire life, everybody treated my father like he was an only child. Dad, Mom, my grandparents. No one mentioned another son," I tell him.

"Why would they do that? Why would they pretend he didn't exist? If it's authentic, that picture shows him with Greg in the last two years. He's been around all this time, but you didn't know about him."

"No," I insist. "I didn't know anything about him. I don't know anything about him. Eric will make sure the picture is authenticated."

"And then?" Sam asks.

Squaring my shoulders to Sam, I stare him directly in the eye, unafraid of the truths hidden there among the questions.

"I find out who that man is, and what he's up to, and plan a little family reunion."

# CHAPTER EIGHT

## LOTAN

FIFTEEN YEARS AGO...

His steps were slow and methodical. They made barely any noise when they touched the ground, which was exactly how he intended it. That took control. It took power and a tight grip to stop all the emotions, the anger, the pain, the grief, from making his feet heavy, so they echoed through the aging building. Levi and Thomas knew he was there, but his silent steps kept them from being able to trace his movements so easily. It gave them just a little bit of hope. Maybe, if they were able to run fast enough, they could get out. But they'd have to find their way first.

Fear is a funny thing. For some, it creates focus. Intense concentration that ensures the one who is afraid can think clearly. They will overcome whatever challenges are in front of them and persevere. They become strong and turn their thoughts and motivations inward so they can push themselves through whatever they need to in order to survive.

Then there are those who can't cope with fear. Rather than getting clearer, their thoughts get tangled and confused. They question themselves, question everything that's going on around them. Their decisions become clouded, and rather than thinking about what they need to do to survive, they panic. Rather than breaking the situation down into the most basic of elements and managing them the way the others do, they become obsessed with the sum totality.

And that's what was happening now. The men probably could have escaped. There were times when he let them get away before. Just to enjoy their sense of fear and know he was making them dangle for just a little bit longer. Just like in that old story, he had them tied to the rack and was forcing them to watch the pendulum swing ever closer. He was letting them feel the blade of the scythe, then pulling it away. Every time he did it, it broke them down just a little more. Took away their strength, their trust. This time, he wasn't going to let them slip away. The time had come.

They could feel it. They knew he was there and had no intention of letting them go. But if they really tried, they might have been able to. If they had thought it through and not let the fear take over, they could have overcome being split up in the belly of the abandoned hotel. Each would have thought about himself and made the logical, calculated choice to make their way through the building and out. But they wouldn't. Each time the pendulum swung made it less likely. Every time he'd let them get close enough to the edge that they could feel the breath of the reaper on their neck, it loosened their grasp on their control of the situation.

Now the two of them scrambled around the dark, grimy building, looking for each other rather than escaping. And so he moved quietly. He wasn't hunting them. They were already caught. But he wanted to savor the fear for just a little longer. He wouldn't have it anymore after this. All he would carry with him were the memories and the satisfaction of his revenge. It would never really be enough. They couldn't atone for what they had done. They had taken something indescribably precious out of the world. They had taken Mariya. And there could never be enough fear, enough pain, enough blood to cleanse them of that.

He took another step. The floorboards groaned beneath him. They'd already been stripped of most of their carpet and padding, so he walked on gritty dust-covered subflooring that was already giving way to the years dragging down on them. At some point, someone had obviously seen some sort of hidden value in the carcass of the hotel. They thought they could save it. Another funny thing about people. Some always have the compulsion to save. Even when there is nothing there to save, hope lingers. Like they can still see the aura of what used to be and think if they only believe in it enough if they put enough into it, they could make those lingering memories solid and real again. Or even transform them into something better.

More often than not, it doesn't work. All the optimism in the world can't drag some things back from disaster. It seemed whoever had started the process of attempting to restore the hotel gave up somewhere along the line. Throughout the building was an uncomfortable dichotomy of distress and progress. Some spaces still held onto the lingering traces of the last people who used them. It was like they just walked away and forgot about the newspaper left sitting on the table beside a floral couch now coated and grayed with dust, or the mail set in a nook behind the desk, never given to the intended recipient. Or even the mug of what could have been a morning coffee set on the marble mantlepiece above the lobby's fireplace.

In other places, all that had been torn down. Carpets ripped up; walls crashed through. Elevators removed from their shafts and the entrances boarded. Signs that whatever team was brought in started in specific areas of the building, but left others untouched. Now it was abandoned again, shuttered, and locked, left to decay.

He knew all of it. Every space. Every room. He'd taken his time to learn it so there would be nowhere the two could hide. Levi and Thomas had been running for just over two years. They began in the softness of spring and would end in the heat of summer. July. When he decided his chase was over and the time was coming, it only seemed appropriate to choose July. These two men ruined Emma's life the night they shot her mother, because they saw a shadow instead of a face, movement instead of eyes. She deserved vengeance, too.

She would never know this is what he did to celebrate her birthday.

They could have kept running. They could have gone anywhere. In the two years they ran, they ventured far across the country. Sometimes they even flourished. They managed to find people who would help them. Sometimes out of the kindness of their own hearts. Sometimes because they were running, too.

But it was the other times that brought them back here. The times that they struggled and clawed for the survival that was barely theirs to claim, anyway. No food, no place to live, no hope. Yet they kept going. Drive for survival at its finest. It was that drive that brought them back. Just as he knew they would be back. Both probably believed they could disappear here just as well, now that time had passed. They would simply melt away into the world's biggest town before he found them.

They underestimated him. Or overestimated themselves. Both were adding sin upon sin.

And so, in the days since he found the men, he set his plans. He took delight in them. They were brought here. Left inside like small animals in a maze. A flicker in the shadows from one side told him one of the men had made it out to this floor. He'd heard the whisper moments before, Levi calling out to Thomas, quietly enough that he hoped he wasn't heard, yet loudly enough to hope he was. He took a step, and in a fraction of a second the man rushed across the small intersection of the hallways in front of him, he caught sight of Levi's face in a slice of moonlight. It was heartbreaking in a way. Those occasional ribbons of mercurial light breaking through the boards covering the windows or slithering around the edges of doors padlocked from the outside was the only light in the hotel. It was the only bit of illumination the men had to guide them, and it betrayed them.

There was no need to hurry. Levi didn't have the control he did, couldn't keep his footsteps quiet on the bare floor. But he ran anyway. Just for the fun of the chase. His blood faster through his veins and triggering the rhythm of his heart. To feel the air on his face and feed off the adrenaline left slick in the air where the man fled from him.

A door crashed behind him, the sound stopping him in his tracks. Now he had a choice. What fun.

He considered which way to go, whether to continue to chase Levi further through the labyrinth of corridors or to follow the sound of the crash, envisioning their positions in the hotel. He wondered if they had found one another already and decided to stay split up so one may have the chance to survive. He doubted it. He knew these men well, understood their motivations. He also knew there were only two directions this could go. Bonds between people either thrive in adversity or collapse because of it. These two would either stop at nothing to find one another, magnetized to each other out of a toxic mix of loyalty and mind-contorting fear, or they would turn on each other, feeding one another to the lions if they had to.

Either would be delightful to see.

For now, he would go for the more exciting catch. He turned away from the sound of Levi's footsteps moving deeper into the building and went in the direction of the crash. A flick of his thumb turned on the beam of his flashlight, and he let it pool at his feet before sweeping it over the walls and into the corners. It only took a few minutes for him to find what he was looking for. A heavy metal door, once cream but now scratched and chipped into a mottled gray, jostled from its position. Not fully open but caught on a piece of debris when it bounced back after crashing closed. It stood just slightly out of place, revealing Thomas's secret.

Careful to keep the piece of debris in place so the door wouldn't automatically lock behind him, he went through and headed up the narrow set of stairs. He counted the floors as he went, listening for the sound of the feet above him. He wondered if Thomas realized what he had done. Maybe he had. Maybe he had a plan still running through his mind. Or maybe he thought the stairwell would have doors to the other floors and only realized his mistake when he was too far up and knew he was being followed.

He heard Thomas go through the final door at the top of the stairs and paused. He didn't want the chase to end too quickly. He wanted to give it just a little bit of time, then have Thomas' fleeting hope wither away like the edges of a rose petal held to a flame. The seconds ticked by. He counted panicked footsteps with them. He couldn't hear them, but he could imagine them. They came along with a look of mounting terror, and only then did he climb the last of the steps and walk through the final door out onto the roof of the hotel.

Thomas whipped around to face him. His eyes widened, and his body swayed as if he wanted to take a step back, but his feet wouldn't cooperate.

"Disappointed?"

"Lotan," Thomas murmured, somewhere between an acknowledgement and a plea.

"Did you think there would be another door? Or perhaps a fire escape? Most of those were taken from buildings years ago, yet people still look for them. But there wouldn't be one coming off the roof. People run to the roof to wait for rescue, not to scramble to the bottom." He took a few steps toward the man. "I suppose if there was really danger and no rescue coming, there would be a choice to be made. Either stay and face it. Or jump off the ledge."

He looked around, taking in the sagging remains of the heating and cooling system and the water tanks. His eyes closed, and his head dropped back as he drew in a breath of the velvety night air, spreading his arms out to the side.

"Sir," Thomas whispered.

He stayed motionless for a long moment. Then he lowered his arms and snapped his eyes open, staring directly at Thomas.

"If I were you, I would choose the ledge."

## CHAPTER NINE

NOW

"It was a shock, to say the least, when Creagan told me he had an undercover assignment for me. For those six months, I'd been doing literally nothing but sitting at a desk shifting papers around. It felt like I was never going to do anything useful ever again and that he was trying to phase me out. Essentially what LaRoche just said about me," I tell Sam.

We've gotten inside the cabin, and I'm still talking through the strange nostalgia creeping in at me from every corner. I'm not sure how I'm supposed to feel right now. It's not happy to be back. That's not it. But there also isn't fear. I'm not afraid of this tiny building or what it represents.

"You know it isn't true," Sam tells me, setting the bags at his feet so he can take me by my shoulders and look into my eyes. "That man is so intimidated by you; he doesn't know how to do anything but try to knock you down a few pegs. It's the only thing that keeps him feeling like he's in charge around here."

"He is in charge around here," I point out. "That's precisely the problem. He's in charge now, and he was in charge when I came here before. Only he didn't know who I was, and so I was able to slither around in his investigation a bit more. Now he knows exactly who I am and why I'm here. He has absolute control, and he loves it. He had it out for me as soon as I got here."

"You just said he didn't know who you were, so you are able to get closer to the investigation," Sam says.

"He didn't know who I was as in he didn't know I was an FBI agent. He did know I was an outsider who quickly proved herself a major annoyance. We set it up, so my undercover persona was that I was trying to find a place to start a new life."

"It's already starting to sound like Sarah Mueller's Ruby Baker story," Sam notices.

I suddenly decide I don't like how having our hastily thrown together bags sitting in the living room feels like an escape hatch, so I pick mine up and carry it into the bedroom.

"Yeah, except she used her boyfriend's connections to take over an empty house, and I ended up in a cabin in the middle of the woods. Well, and she was on the brink of becoming a serial killer, and I was here to stop one," I note.

"An important distinction," Sam shrugs, following me and setting the rest of our stuff on the bed beside the bag I carried.

"It is. As is the one between abandoned and rarely used," I say.

"What do you mean?" he asks.

"When we first rented the cabin for me to stay in, it was because Creagan wanted to make sure I was close to the action. Feathered Nest is a pretty small place, so it's not like there are tons of hotels and Airbnbs sitting around available. He found this place on a property listing and was told it was abandoned, but available for use. But when I had Clancy over to repair the furnace, he made a point to mention the town owns the cabin and rents it out to people visiting the area. I'm definitely not the first person to stay here, and it wasn't really abandoned. He told me, Wendy, the woman who lived here died, and the property was never claimed," I say.

"Wait," Sam frowns. "The woman who lived here, as in Jake's grandmother?"

"Now you're catching on. Granted, nobody knew she was his grandmother or that he spent time here. But it's why the property wasn't claimed. Wendy and her daughter—Jake's mother—did not get on well at all, and when Wendy died, she never came forward to claim it. Wendy practically disowned her when she married John, Jake's father. John was far from being an upstanding pillar of Feathered Nest society. Everybody in town knew him, and Wendy knew the type of person her daughter was and the way they mistreated Jake. Staying out of their way meant being able to protect Jake and not being humiliated by her own daughter. Years before her death, she told Clancy she had a daughter but didn't see her anymore. I'm sure that's exactly how she felt."

"So, who actually rented it to you?" Sam asks.

"I never actually found out. The landlord was supposed to be waiting for me when I got here. I had been traveling for more than a day. Creagan had me going all over hell and back on the trains to create confusion and make it harder to trace a direct line between my arrival in Feathered Nest and where I came from. He had a car waiting for me at the train station, and it took me another forty-five minutes just to get here."

"How far is the train station?" Sam asks. "There wasn't a parking lot there that I saw."

"Not that one," I say. "I wasn't coming on a train from the direction of Quantico or Sherwood, so I ended up at a different train station than the one we did. Anyway, when I got here, there was nobody to be seen. A key was hanging on the front door, and that was my welcome. At least until someone knocked on the door, and when I opened it, a man fell dead at my feet."

"Ron Murdock," Sam nods.

"Only I didn't find his name out until later. He had no identification or anything with him. All he had was a piece of paper with my name written on it in his hand. And a gunshot wound to his back. So, dealing with that was LaRoche's first encounter with me. Even though I had just gotten here that night, it was obvious he was suspicious. I can only imagine how much more suspicious he would have been if he saw the paper."

"You never even told him about it?"

I shake my head and open my bag to start pulling things out so we can put them away. Creating some sense of normalcy in the cabin might smooth out the sharp edges of just how twisted it was for LaRoche to send me back here to stay during the investigation into Marren Purcell's death. He wanted it to get to me, but I wasn't going to let it.

"No. It had my real name on it. Emma Griffin, not Emma Monroe. The undercover assignment before this one didn't go well for me. Showing the local cop my real name on a piece of paper in the hand of a man murdered within minutes of me getting to town would have blown that cover fully to shit. Besides, it felt too personal to share with them. Remember, I wasn't in the right state of mind at the time. Now, if I found something like that, I would obviously get some backup on it."

"Like now?" Sam asks.

"Exactly. The paper, the notes on the train, the messages with Marren. They're all about me. And I told the police. It's still on me to finish this, to figure it out, and bring this guy down. But as much as it is about me, I can't pretend it doesn't have to do with the rest of the world, too. They aren't game pieces; they're people."

"You're right. And they deserve justice for their deaths," he adds.

Carrying an armful of clothes, I cross to the dresser and pull open a middle drawer. A gasp forms and dies in my throat when I look inside. The old, worn fabric is just as soft beneath my fingertips as when I was here a year ago. Sam's words sink in, and I pull the quilt from the drawer to make space.

"That's bullshit," I say.

"How can you say that as a law enforcement agent?" he asks. "The point of your job is to find justice for the victims of crimes."

I stuff my clothes into the drawer and bring my toiletries into the bathroom.

"There is no justice when someone is murdered," I reply, walking back into the bedroom. "Justice means making something fair and balanced. Justice is when a bullied little boy grows up to be the powerful head of a company that employs everyone who tormented him. Justice is when a girl musters up the courage to ask a gorgeous guy out and is mocked and turned down, only for years later to be beautiful and see him miserable, ugly, and alone. Justice is when someone steals from a store, and they have to work there to pay the debt. Where is that for someone who is stabbed through the heart, or dismembered and shoved in a box? How do you make it fair and balanced for a child suffocated in a hammock or a woman with her throat slashed in her living room? The idea of getting justice for a murder victim is bullshit. As a law enforcement agent, it's my job to make people like that pay for as long as possible while they wait for the day they die and face real justice."

"And involving the police from the start will help you do that," Sam says reassuringly. He knows I'm struggling with being kept at a distance, with not being able to control the investigation and carry it where I need to.

"It will also help keep the bodies from stacking up with a sticky note that says 'Emma did it'. I've had my taste of being accused of murder, and I don't need any more of it. I will happily leave that to Jessica Fletcher from *Murder, She Wrote*."

"Jessica Fletcher?" Sam asks with a laugh. "You've been watching too many of those old shows."

"You know everybody thought she did it," I tell him. "She lived in the country's tiniest town, and yet every other day somebody wound up murdered. And who was always there? Jessica, the retired teacher, trying to look all innocent with her sweaters and her glasses hanging from a necklace."

I stop. Mentioning the character was meant to lighten the heaviness, to keep Sam and me from cracking. But the image I painted reminded me of something else. I rush out of the bedroom and back out onto the porch. Sam follows me, nearly tumbling from the open front door like he's unsure what I'll do if I'm out of his sight.

"What are you doing?" he asks.

"The necklace," I say.

"Jessica Fletcher's necklace?"

"No. Mine. Mine and my mother's. You saw the picture of us wearing them when I was little. One was left in my house in Quantico on my birthday before I went back to Sherwood. Clancy mailed the other one to me after he found it under the porch."

"Right. That one must have been in Ron Murdock's pocket and slipped through the cracks in the wood when he fell," Sam says.

"Yes. Only… " I reach into my shirt and pull out the necklace I've taken to wearing since seeing the picture. Taking it off, I hold it down close to the porch. "It won't fit."

Sam crouches down and looks at where I'm holding the necklace. The pendant is clearly too large to fit through the gaps between the slats of the porch, and there are no holes or other gaps nearby.

"And you're sure they didn't replace the porch or anything? Maybe they repaired it and brought the slats closer together?" he asks.

I shake my head. "No. Look at the color of the wood. It's weathered and aged. It's exactly like the rest of the porch and the pillars. And if you look closely enough, you can still see traces of his blood where it soaked in before they could clean it. This is the porch where he died. But unless he took the necklace out of his pocket and threw it under the porch before knocking, Ron Murdock isn't the one who put it there."

## CHAPTER TEN

"Somehow, I doubt a man dying of a gunshot wound would think about taking a necklace out of his pocket just to toss it under a porch," Sam says.

"So do I," I nod. "Not that I haven't seen people do some pretty extraordinary things in the moments right before death, but this doesn't strike me as something he did. He would have no way of knowing anybody was going to look under the porch. If he wanted me to find it or to see it, he could have just left it in his pocket. Or taken it out and had it in his hand. It doesn't make any sense for him to put it under the porch, and there's no way it fell down between the slats."

"And the other necklace isn't smaller?" he asks.

"Smaller?" I ask.

"One of them is yours, and one is your mother's. You wore them together when you were a little girl. Is yours the same scale as hers, or smaller?"

"The same," I tell him." I don't even know which one of these I wore and which my mother wore. But the thing is, Clancy mentioned they had just cleaned out under that porch a little bit before I was here the first time. It was unusual to go to the effort of cleaning out under it frequently, but after the murder, they wanted to make sure there wasn't any blood under the porch to attract animals. And that's how they found the necklace. So, it couldn't have been there for long."

"So, Ron Murdock probably didn't have anything to do with the necklaces at all," Sam notes.

"It doesn't seem that way," I say, a disquieting blend of shock and disappointment filling me.

Ever since finding out about the necklaces, they've been a connection between Ron Murdock and this whole situation. It's upsetting that I still have no idea who he was and why he was in Feathered Nest the night I got there. Even the tiniest clue, the smallest link could help me feel less like I'm completely missing something. But I obviously am.

Sam reaches over to run his hand along my back.

"You knew he couldn't have had anything to do with the first necklace. You got it, what, five months after he died? He couldn't have been the one to put that one in your house. That has always meant there was more than one person involved. Now you can consider if it might have been just one," he says.

"Which is better, trying to will myself into believing Murdock stole a couple of celestial ponies and pulled a ghostly express to bring me the first necklace after he did drop the one found later? Or wrapping my head around a nameless, faceless person knowing where I lived, was able to get in without being noticed, and also came to Feathered Nest where they knew where I stayed?" I ask.

"Knowing it was likely only one person helps to narrow it," he points out. "Rather than two people trying to give you a message with the necklaces, or one trying to tell you about the other, it's just one."

"This man, whoever he actually was, is the only new link I've had to my parents in a long time," I explain. "I should know him. I should know why he would be here, but now I feel even further from that."

"He is still a link to your parents," Sam says. "You know he knew them. You've seen the picture."

"It's more than that," I say.

"What do you mean?" he asks.

"It's not just the picture of him with my parents. It's not even the link to Iowa. That's tangible proof, but I know there's more. I have memories of him. At least, I think it's him. It being him is the only thing that makes sense, but at the same time, it doesn't because I still don't know who he is or why he would be there."

"What kind of memories?" Sam asks. "Did you meet him or talk to him?"

"Nothing that concrete. It's just... flashes. It's like I have memories of these little moments in my life, and when I just think about them, all I can see is that memory. Like I'm focused in on it and see only that moment. But if I look around the edges, I find him. And it keeps happening. I keep discovering him in memories I've gone over so many times in my mind. It's like he's always there, I just never realized it. He was at the waterpark on a day I was there with Dad. I remember sitting on one of those lounge chairs eating French fries and a sno-cone. Mom was there somewhere. I know she was. But all I can remember is Dad. He was sitting on the chair beside mine, and he stole some of my fries. That's usually where the memory stopped. I didn't think about anything past that. But then I thought about it further and remembered him looking up. Not anything big, not a really noticeable gesture like he was surprised or looking for something. Just a really slight movement. So, I looked up and saw a man a few yards away. He wasn't in a bathing suit like everybody else. He looked at us like he knew us."

"Did you know him?" Sam asks.

"That's the thing. I can't really tell. It's like I do, but I don't. Like I recognized him as someone I've seen before, but not as a specific person. There are a few memories like that. Where that man just kind of exists on the periphery of what's happening, and nobody acknowledges he's there. Not in a negative way, like they're trying to ignore him or don't want him to be there. They just don't say anything about him or go over and talk to him. It's like he's there and he's not at the same time. But that's what kind of makes me worry about it."

"What do you mean worry about it?"

"What if I'm not actually remembering him? What if I saw that picture and have just started superimposing him into various moments in my life, but he wasn't actually there?"

"Are all the memories the same?" Sam asks. "Is he wearing the same thing? Have the same mannerisms?"

"No. It's different for each of the memories."

"Then I don't think that's what's happening. If you were just layering him in there, you wouldn't have that much variety. It's possible, I guess. You're the most imaginative person I've ever known, so if there was going to be someone whose brain would do that, it would be you. But I think it's much more likely you have real memories of him. He was obviously fairly close with your parents. That picture looks pretty chummy. And you were around during that time. That wasn't taken before you were born. It makes sense you might have seen him around," Sam tells me.

"Then why wouldn't I remember meeting him? Or spending any time with him? There are no memories of interacting with him. Any of us. He's just there," I say.

"Is there anything else consistent about the memories? Anything else you can think of that links those specific moments?"

I think about this for a few seconds, letting my brain bounce from moment to moment. Just like I told Sam, these are moments I have thought about so many times over the years without ever noticing that man in them. Now that he's surfacing in them, it makes me wonder how many other memories have him in them and I just haven't yet discovered him. Something occurs to me, the longer I think about it. It's tenuous, but at this point, everything is.

"Every time I think of a memory with Ron Murdock, whoever he is, in it, it's right before one of Dad's trips. Like the one I was just telling you about where I was at the waterpark. He left the next day and was gone for a few weeks."

"Did you know where he was?" Sam asks.

"No, I never did. But Mom wasn't concerned about it and just told me he would be back, like always. And he was. It wasn't always long stretches like that. There were times when he was only gone for a couple of days. But whenever a memory pops up that has Murdock in it, my father left soon after."

"Emma, could he have been your father's handler?"

The concept of my father having a handler was always abstract to me. I grew up knowing he was in the CIA and that his job meant doing difficult and often dangerous things he couldn't talk about. Just as I had to be accustomed to moving around all the time and never being completely sure what was happening at any moment of my childhood, I had to accept that I would never know many of the details about my father's career. The older I got and the more I understood about his agency as well as the Bureau, the more I learned about the intricacies that existed within the organizations. One being the existence of handlers.

These specialized officers are assigned to agents to act as a buffer between the agents and the organization itself. Rather than an agent engaging directly with the organization to receive instructions or transfer intelligence, the handler acts as a go-between. They are often referred to as cut-outs because their interaction with the agents cuts out the need for them to engage with other agents or with the larger organization.

"I don't know," I tell Sam. "Dad never mentioned having a handler, and that picture made it look like Murdock was very friendly with my parents. Friendlier than I would expect that type of professional relationship to be."

"How long was he around?" Sam asks. "When is your last memory of him?"

I let out a long breath and look at the wood porch in front of me again. Resting my hand where his body lay, I try to connect with the man I knew only as Ron Murdock. I try to let it trace back to create a thread that will draw me back through each moment of my life when he was there. But those moments are jumbled, out of order, and I don't know how to arrange them into place.

## CHAPTER ELEVEN

### MURDOCK

SEVENTEEN YEARS AGO...

He should have been there. As soon as he had a feeling something was wrong, he should have acted. He would never forgive himself for that. He would never again be able to look in a mirror and accept what he saw because there would always be blood on his hands, and the image in his eyes would never go away. Whenever he looked at himself, he would see her. Even more, he would see Ian. Reflected in his eyes, he would see Ian's face staring back at him through the splash of the lights that dissolved away the midnight darkness along that hidden road.

Ian gave absolutely no indication that Murdock was even there. He made no move, no gesture. Nothing to communicate through the crowd. Murdock waited to hear something. He was still waiting. The trucks were gone, the cars that clogged the road disentangled from their self-created jam so they could slide away to the next scene, the next moment of chaos. Ian was already gone. Packed up in his blue-striped pajamas into the back of the ambulances so he could sit alongside Mariya one last time. There would be no sirens. There would be no CPR or life support. They weren't here to rescue. They were here only to collect.

The men in dark suits were also gone. They had lingered in the house long after the stretcher was pulled through the entryway and brought out into the night air. They stayed after Ian left, and after the responding officers swept the area. Murdock stayed out of sight. He remained on the edge, not bringing any attention to himself until they were gone.

Emma was still there. Lost in the turmoil and upheaval of the night, she was left behind in a house that now felt so much quieter than it had before. No one went upstairs to wake her or to find out if she saw or heard anything. Many of them probably didn't even realize she was there. But she couldn't remain alone. There was no way of knowing how long Ian would be gone or what may happen between the time the hidden road in front of the house emptied, and he returned.

When they were all gone, Murdock walked into the house through the side door and surveyed what was left. Very little had changed about the space. Most people who saw it wouldn't think very much was different. But he could see the tatters of life that once existed. He could feel the shift, the oppressive weight now hovering in each of the rooms. For a second, he considered climbing the stairs and looking in on Emma. Just a quick glance to make sure she was alright. Something told him she hadn't actually slept through the entire event. She was young, but not a baby or toddler who would be able to block out anything happening in the world around them to get sleep. It seemed unlikely an almost twelve-year-old girl would make it peacefully through her mother being murdered on the floor of the house just beneath her.

He stopped himself. Now wasn't the time, and he wasn't the person to talk to her about what happened. She didn't know him. He knew her, of course. He had known her from the time she was born. But Emma didn't know him. That was by design. Planned before she even came into the world. She would never know. She couldn't know who he was or who her parents truly were. There was always the agreement that one day they would be completely honest with her. When she was old enough to fully understand it and make the decisions for herself, they would tell her the truth. None of it would make sense to her before then, and Ian and Mariya didn't want to give her a glimpse into a world she wasn't ready to fully know. She wasn't yet ready to know the aspects of her life that he lived in. So, she couldn't know him.

But the time would come. At least, that's what they always said. The time would come when she would be ready, and they could tell her. From there, it would be her choice of what to do with the information.

But that time would never come. Not now.

He went into the living room and sat down, turning on the TV to drown out the silence. A cascade of brightly colored jellybeans spilled down from the corner of the screen onto a bed of glistening green Easter grass as a pale brown bunny hopped into view, nose twitching as if to remind parents of the upcoming holiday.

"If you haven't gotten your candy yet, time is running out!"

"Don't forget to fill the eggs and stuff the baskets so they'll be ready Sunday morning!"

"Set the alarm to wake up before the sun and hide the eggs for curious fingers to find!"

"It will soon be time for the big hunt!"

Above him, Murdock heard the sound of shifting movements hovering just at the top of the stairs. He didn't turn to look. If Emma wanted to come down, she would. But she didn't.

It was already time for the hunt. But they weren't seeking out vibrant plastic shells filled with fanciful treats tucked in the bushes, forgotten in the ivy to be discovered weeks down the line. They were hunting for a monster.

He stayed for several hours until a message on his phone told him Ian had left the office and was heading home. The message wasn't from Ian. Murdock didn't expect it to be. More time would have to pass before then.

He slipped out of the side door of the house so he wouldn't be noticed and walked away.

## CHAPTER TWELVE

NOW

We're starting back into the cabin when a sound stops me. The February night is cold and far too chilly for the animals of the woods around the cabin to be out roaming. The temperature dropped significantly after the sun went down, and even though spring is coming, they would know to forage for food earlier in the day to catch the last of the warmth. They shouldn't be walking so close to the cabin.

Yet there's the sound. A distinct crack of a branch and shuffling in the leaves. Sam and I pause, looking at each other. My hand touches his arm as if creating a connection would keep us safer.

"What was that?" he asks in a soft whisper.

I nod slightly toward the back of the cabin.

"It sounds like there's someone in the woods," I say.

Memories flood me, but I don't let them take over. Instead, I carefully step toward the door to the cabin. We left it standing slightly open when we came out onto the porch, so it's easy to slip back inside. But I have no intention of locking the door, pulling down the shades, and hiding away. Instead, I walked purposefully into the bedroom, pull a second of my bags up onto the bed and open it.

"You stay here," Sam says. "I'm going to go check it out."

"Not a chance," I tell him. "You've never been here. You don't know those woods like I do. Besides, the last time I was here, I ran into those woods in the middle of the night with nothing but an idea and a whole lot of recklessness." I turn around with my freshly loaded gun in my hand. "Nothing's going to keep me out this time."

We step back out onto the porch and pause to listen. I don't hear anything for a few seconds. Then I hear it. Another crack deeper in the woods. If there is somebody near the cabin, they're trying to slink away. Not bothering with the wooden steps, I jump down from the porch and take off into the woods. Sam rushes after me, and I hear him prep his gun. A beam of light glows from behind me, and I know he's taken out his flashlight. I didn't bother to get mine. Both of us with full hands puts us at a disadvantage if we do find someone back here.

I'm careful to walk as much on the beaten-down path as I possibly can to avoid walking across the piles of dried leaves and branches. It's not lost on me that the path is much wider and more tightly packed than it was when I was here a year ago. Back then, these woods were rarely used. Rumors and legends surrounded the woods and told of darkness existing within them. The older folks of town whispered about a house that once stood among the trees. None of them knew just how true those myths really were.

But now that the truth about Jake's family home was revealed, the curious and morbid came from all over to sample the atmosphere and build their own stories. So many claimed to be disgusted and repelled by man's inhumanity to man. It's a theme, a trope, a personality trait of vigorous virtue signalers everywhere. But the reality is, people are fascinated by it. Blood and trauma and tragedy draw them in. Whether it's because it makes them feel alive or out of some sense of responsibility to not forget the dead or some twisted pleasure that comes from it, horrific situations are never short spectators and celebrants.

We go deeper into the woods, listening intently for retreating footsteps. As we get closer to the house, I start to notice little bits of color on the ground in front of me. I pause so Sam can catch up, and the beam of his flashlight shines down on the path in front of me. It's flowers. Not growing up from the ground, but instead cut and scattered there. Torn and ground down by footsteps and animals. I follow the petals, watching their coverage become thicker and more consistent as we pass through the trees. Soon they become flowers again until I notice pieces of ravaged bouquets and even broken pots, their soil and roots and stems spilling out on the ground in scattered, disturbed piles.

"What the hell is this?" Sam asks.

I gesture ahead of us.

"Jake's house," I say. "Just up the way through the thickest part of the trees. These must have been left as tributes by visitors and then either scattered by vandals or animals."

"How is it not blocked off from the public?" Sam asks. "I would think they wouldn't want anybody getting anywhere near something like that."

"I would think they'd want to bulldoze it to the ground," I say. "But it's not that easy. You know that as well as I do. They removed the bodies, of course. And boarded it up. The fire damaged it so much it's dangerous to even get near, but until the case is completely over, they're not going to destroy it. He's already in prison for some of the charges, but there are plenty more. If there are technicalities or appeals, anything that might even for a second get him out; he'll get scooped right back up."

"So, the house still stands there," Sam says.

"Yes," I nod. "And short of armed officers positioned around the perimeter to stop anyone from getting even close to it, there's nothing anyone can do to stop people from coming to it. The thing is, it's not just the gore-porn aspect of it. There are plenty of faked pictures and blurred crime scene images available to give them that kick. Some of the people who come here are looking for that kind of thrill, sure, but that's not all of them. The ones who come here, who leave flowers, they genuinely feel connected to the people who died here. They can sense that loss and despair. Some even grieve for Jake."

"Why would anyone have any sympathy for somebody like him? He killed more than fourteen people. He tore them up and stuffed them like trophies to create his twisted museum display," Sam points out, a distinct note of disgust in his voice.

"That's true. But those people will argue he did those things because he's a victim of the life he was forced to live. Everything that happened to him chipped away at his ability to be a normal human and crafted him into what he became. Whether that's what happened or not, and whether he's deserving of any kind of sympathy or empathy or not isn't the point. The point is these people feel it strongly and are drawn to come here and experience it. They don't want what happened here to be forgotten or to just fade away."

"I don't think I'll ever understand something like that," Sam mutters.

I glance over at him.

"What is the strongest proof that there's something more than us, something bigger?" I ask.

"You mean God?" he asks.

"God. Gods. Goddesses. The Universe. The Spirits. Whatever anyone wants to call it, and whatever they believe it is, what is the strongest proof that it exists?"

He shakes his head slightly. "Love?"

"That's what everyone says. But I don't buy it. The things we call love, loyalty, compassion, friendship, bonding… they are all easy to link to survival. You feel that sense of connection to others because they will protect you, and you will protect them. You feel it to your partner so you will mate and reproduce. You feel it to your young, so you will take care of them. It means more than that on an emotional level, of course, but if you try to break it down and analyze its purpose, that's what you have. God gives love and shows love, but that's not the proof."

"Then what is?"

"Grief."

"Your proof of a higher power is grief?" Sam asks. "Being sad?"

"Yes. People find joy and happiness in the things more likely to keep them healthy, safe, and strong. Food. Fun. Relaxation. Sex. Friendship. Those feelings are rewards that keep you motivated and surviving. People don't grieve to survive. Purely from a survival perspective, if a member of your group dies, you find someone else to fill their role. If your partner dies, you find someone else to reproduce with. You don't grieve. Some say sadness is to motivate you to not lose what makes you happy, but that isn't true. You don't try to protect your children because you don't want to be sad. You protect them because you love them and want to take care of them. And it doesn't explain this."

I gesture to the flowers on the ground. "These are strangers coming here because they grieve for people they don't even know. They feel the tear in humanity, the open wound every one of us shares when someone is ripped unfairly from life. We feel that because there is more to life than survival."

## CHAPTER THIRTEEN

### LOTAN

FIFTEEN YEARS AGO ...

No one would ever hear Thomas's screams. That was probably the best part. They were so far out, so far from any people and surviving businesses, it didn't matter how loud he was. His voice could creep higher and louder, echo out into the stars, and it would still mean nothing. It would never reach anyone. Even if there was someone who happened by and heard the traces of his cries, they wouldn't know what it was. They could just as easily think it was the angry scream of a mountain lion or the final, gasping cries of an animal caught in its jaws. Nothing they would pay any mind to.

Not that it mattered. They could know exactly what it was. They could recognize the desperate, agonized screams of a man paying his debt for cutting down the most beautiful, most treasured woman ever to walk the earth. Even if they did, there was no way they would get to him in time. They could come into the broken, overgrown parking lot of the hotel and see exactly what was happening. They could watch the metal claw he wielded slice through Thomas's skin and drag it from the bones. They could see his terrified, blood-soaked hands grasp the edge of the building and try to climb his way over.

After all, that's what Lotan offered him. In those first moments on the roof, he told him he had the option to go over the ledge. He could escape Lotan's rage that way if that was his choice. But Thomas stayed where he was. He did everything he could not to make eye contact while still carefully watching Lotan and his movements so he could have some chance of responding to them. He never would. He never had that chance. As much as he thought he did— really, as soon as he stepped foot in the hotel—he was breathing air into a corpse.

And so, it didn't matter at all if someone came. It didn't even really matter if Levi somehow found his way out of the building and ran. These moments on the roof were worth it. After all, Thomas was the one holding the gun that day two years before. When the two men walked away from him, on their way to fulfill the mission he entrusted them with, it was Thomas who left with the weapon already in his hand. He was determined and driven, ready for the challenge that presented itself to him.

And now he would pay for that.

To give the fool credit, he did try to escape. His devotion and loyalty were strong enough to keep him in place for several long seconds, facing off against the leader to which he had once deferred all things. But that drive—that internal, involuntary need for survival—won out, and Thomas turned to run for the door that led back down into the hallway. They were just far enough away that Lotan had the time to pull the chain from the bag on his shoulder. One swing was enough to plant the vicious metal points into the base of Thomas's neck. He didn't scream. Not in that moment.

The shock of that first impact was so intense Thomas's mind couldn't process what his body was going through. He could only stop, his back stiff, his eyes locked on the door he couldn't reach. His hands moved slightly to the side, his fingers spreading out, like the jolts moving along his nerve endings were shooting out from his fingertips.

Lotan yanked on the chain, sending Thomas tumbling off his feet.

The spikes weren't embedded deeply enough in his upper spine to stay as he pulled the chain back toward him. They pried out of the muscle and clawed down his skin as Thomas fought against it. But it was no use. He crashed hard across the rough concrete of the roof. Lotan took the chain back into his hands and gripped it so he could swing it overhead. The heft was satisfying in his hands. He released mid-swing and let the claw catch Thomas again.

The man was starting to crawl toward the door, but the metal spikes stopped him. This time they dug into the small of his back, crushing through bone and splattering blood in the moonlight. Thomas cried out, his hands digging at the roof to either side of him in desperation to find something to grab as if it would help him. This time yanking the chain back brought Thomas with it. It dragged him across the ground, so the course concrete of the roof scraped at his skin and pulled away clothes. The punctures in his spine kept him from moving quickly enough to have any chance of getting away. Thomas' eyes moved desperately to the ledge of the roof. His wish was evident in that stare. He longed for the release of flight. Even if only for a few moments, he would have been at peace.

Lotan felt fulfilled by each blow. Vindicated by the blood. Flesh tore from bones and screams turned to gurgles, then to gasps, then to silence. Anyone could have come at any moment, and Lotan wouldn't have cared. He wouldn't have stopped or tried to hide. There was no shame in what he was doing, no fear in what they could do to him in return. There was nothing anyone could do that was worse than the torment he already faced, or bad enough to make this not worth it. He'd been waiting two years, and he would happily offer himself up in return if that's what it cost.

Of course, that's not what he wanted. Thomas was only part of this. A piece of the dreams that kept him up at night for two years. If he could only revel in this, he would accept it. It would be enough for him to enjoy these moments and then join Mariya. But if he could have more, he wanted it. There was still one more. He'd listened closely to the sounds around him, waiting for anything that might tell him Levi had gotten out of the hotel. But he heard nothing. He saw nothing.

The screams were probably enough to paralyze him. From what he'd already shown, those sounds wouldn't propel him out of the disintegrating hotel. They would terrify him into hiding. That meant Lotan had time. He could enjoy his time with Thomas, then go look for Levi. He hoped he could find him. He had so many more plans.

When he was finished, he dragged what was left of Thomas over to the ledge. The years on the run hadn't been kind to the man. He was much smaller than before. It made it easier to pull him up onto the top of the wall. Lotan looked over the edge, ensuring he was in just the right spot. He was very familiar with the surroundings of the hotel, and a thought flitted playfully through his mind when he remembered the pool. Taking the claws from Thomas a final time, he gave the man a push and let him drop.

Lotan rolled the chain back up and tucked the metal spikes away in his bag. The weapon resembled a heavier, more menacing grappling hook. He latched it over the side of the wall. He swung his body over and moved down the side of the building. This was far from the first time he'd gotten off a roof this way, and his feet hit the pool deck with smooth control. He left the hook where it was hanging from the roof. Maybe he would reclaim it. Maybe he would leave it hanging there to be found.

Right now, he was only thinking about the body stretched out on the cement a few feet away. When he'd first explored this hotel, he'd noticed the pool. Carved deep into the cement, it had been left without any cover or protection when the hotel was abandoned. In fact, it looked like it was forgotten when the final hotel employees shut it down, and when the team that came to revitalize it decided to walk away. Rather than being drained and lined with a tarp the way he'd seen done before, the pool still stood full of water. Green with algae, dark and murky, it sat still and stagnant without the benefit of the filtration system and being constantly fed by the rain. Leaves and bits of debris drifted idly on top of the thick algae cover, and occasionally it formed itself into eerie shapes as if something had taken over and was lurking in the depths.

Lotan walked up to Thomas. The man's body lay crumpled and contorted, his head crushed by the cement. A single shove with the sole of his boot against the back of his shoulder started him over the edge of the pool. Another made him slip through the surface. The last part visible, his bloody fingers, slid across the deck before disappearing into the cloudy darkness.

## CHAPTER FOURTEEN

NOW

Sam and I walk around the woods for a few minutes more, trying to find who or what made the sound behind the cabin. I am positive it was a person. I know the sound of two feet in boots compared to the paws or hooves of the creatures who live among the trees. There was somebody there. They got close enough to the cabin for us to hear them from the porch, which means they were only feet away from the pool of light cast by the motion detector attached to the side of the cabin.

That thought makes me shudder. I shake off the feeling and the image of Jake installing the light on that cloudy day. The shards of glass left over from the previous fixture being destroyed were still scattered across the backseat of my car, where I discovered them. It was a nice touch and distracted me just briefly. When he'd first put up the light, it felt protective, like he wanted to make sure I stayed safe by chasing away anyone who might come close to the cabin.

Now I can only see that light as a way to make sure he could see me. But that doesn't matter anymore. It wasn't Jake creeping around among the trees. The grotesque warning in the note left on our car aside, Jake is still in prison. He's under close watch, and there's no way he could have slipped away from them to orchestrate all of this without someone noticing. Not that I think he is the type to have done it anyway. That's not how his mind works. Catch Me wants to play games. Jake hunted.

Regardless of how confident I feel someone was definitely in the trees watching me, we don't find anything. We make our way back to the cabin, and when we get to the porch, I immediately notice the door standing slightly open. We pause on the bottom step, and I gesture toward it with a slight nod.

"That was closed," I say.

I meant it as a question, wanting him to contradict me and say I'm remembering wrong. But it comes out as a declaration. Because I know Sam shut the door tightly behind us. He always does. It's everything I can do to stop him from changing the locks on my house in Sherwood every few weeks. If he had his way, every entry point to my home would look like Fort Knox. There's no way he would leave the door to the cabin open even slightly.

"Not only was it closed, it was locked," Sam nods, tightening his grip on his gun.

I nod and lift my gun as I push the door the rest of the way open. When nothing immediately launches at me, I go the rest of the way in. Everything seems exactly as we left it. I don't notice anything out of place or obviously moved. There's nothing new or unusual placed on any of the surfaces. We make our way further into the cabin and explore, sweeping through every corner, making sure there's no one there.

"Living room's clear," I call out.

"Bedroom's clear. Hallway, too," Sam replies.

We carefully comb through every room, hearts hammering in our chests, calling out to each other to mark each room safe. But there's no one there. No sign of the space being compromised.

"Why would somebody unlock and open the door and then do nothing?" I ask once we're back in the living room with all the lights on.

"I don't know," Sam says, shaking his head. "It's entirely possible it was somebody from town. Maybe the guy LaRoche had give us the key didn't get a chance to tell everybody the cabin is being used, and they came by to check something or even use it themselves. Maybe it was the Clancy guy you talk about."

"Clancy would have no reason to come over here without somebody calling him. They already did repairs and updates after everything happened. Besides, if it was somebody from town, don't you think they would notice our car sitting in the driveway? And why would they leave the door open?" I point out.

Before he gets a chance to answer, I hear footsteps coming up on the porch. They're heavy and obvious, not the footsteps of somebody trying to cover their presence there. Sam and I scramble up from the couch, our weapons at the ready, just as we hear a solid, forceful knock in the middle of the door.

Sam looks over at me.

"Expecting someone?" he whispers.

I gesture toward the door.

"Last time I opened it on my first night in Feathered Nest, there was a dead man on the other side. Your turn."

Sam puts one hand on the doorknob, the other raised with his gun.

"Identify yourself," Sam calls, his voice deep.

"Feathered Nest police," a voice says from the other side of the door.

Sam glances back over his shoulder at me, and I step up beside him.

"What's your name?" I ask.

"Miss Griffin, it's Nicolas," he announces.

I resist the urge to roll my eyes. I manage it, but the sheer effort of my restraint aches in the muscles in the backs of them.

"Stand down," I sigh, pressing Sam's shoulder, so he takes a step back from the door. "I know this one."

Opening the door to the young officer is several degrees short of a happy reunion. The same judgmental eyes I dealt with the last time I was here stare at me from the porch, almost daring me to try to fool him again.

"Miss Griffin," he says again like he wants to make sure I know he's aware of my real name.

"That's Agent Griffin," I correct him. If he's going to get it right, he's going to get it right on both accounts. "What are you doing here?"

"This is Sheriff Johnson?" Nicolas asks.

"Yes," I say. "What are you doing here?"

"Chief assigned me to you," he explains.

"Excuse me?" I ask.

"You'll be shadowing me during the investigation."

I cringe against the response I really want to give and offer a tense smile.

"Of course I will," I mutter. "Who else would he assign me to?"

Out of the corner of my eye, I notice Sam looking at me strangely.

"I was on the investigation into the murders and disappearances the last time she was here," Nicolas explains.

"Ah," Sam nods. It pretty much sums everything up.

"Did you just come by to let me know that?" I ask.

"Actually, I would like to talk to you about the investigation. I know you just got to town and are probably settling in, but if you have a few minutes to spare, I'd appreciate it," Nicolas says.

He sounds sincere, at least as sincere as he's capable of, past his arrogance and obvious distrust of me. But right now, the way he's talking to me doesn't really matter. If he's willing to talk about the case, I want to hear all of it. Stepping back from the door, I gesture for him to come inside.

"Can I get you something to drink?" I ask.

"Coffee?"

"Is that because you enjoy it or because it's going to be a long night?" I ask.

He sits down on the couch and looks directly at me.

"Coffee," he repeats.

There are no voices coming from the living room as I dig through the cabinets in the kitchen, hoping to find something. When I offered the drink, it didn't occur to me that I haven't gone to the grocery store, and since they weren't anticipating me being here, it's unlikely anybody stocked the kitchen. Fortunately, it seemed there are some basics that just exist anytime there's the possibility of people, and I'm able to find a jar of instant coffee. Unscrewing the top and smelling the stale, freeze-dried crystals, I change my assertion to unfortunately.

With no other option, I stir a few spoonful's of the fairly offensive pseudo-coffee into hot water and carry it into the living room.

"I don't have any cream or sugar," I tell him. "We didn't exactly come into this prepared."

"I don't think anybody could prepare for what happened today," Nicolas says. "And I'm sure you understand the gravity of It."

"Do I understand the gravity of a woman split open like a fish in the middle of her living room floor and my name written across the wall in her blood? Yeah. I understand the gravity of it," I snap.

Nicolas looks down at his hands with a sarcastic grin, then up at me again.

"What can you tell me about that?" he asks.

"What do you mean?"

"You called Chief LaRoche several days ago asking him to check in on Marren to make sure she was alright. She had told everyone she was visiting with her sister out of town, and she wasn't expected back yet. But conveniently, you're the one who discovers her body," he says.

"Conveniently? You call what happened earlier today convenient?" I say.

"You have to admit it seems strange," he counters.

"No. What seems strange is that I have to deal with this shadowing bullshit at all. Maybe you're not aware of the case I'm already involved in, that started because of the note that made me call LaRoche to begin with, but there are three other people dead, and there are going to be more if this doesn't end."

"I'm aware of it," he says. "And it only makes this investigation more urgent. So, I need you to tell me what you know, and we'll go from there."

## CHAPTER FIFTEEN

"What is it that you think I know?" I ask. "Because I have a strong feeling you're trying to ask me something without asking me."

"I just want to know what you do about this investigation. You said it yourself; you're already involved in a case you seem to believe is linked to this one. If you can provide us any information about it, it could be very helpful," Nicolas says.

"I don't 'seem to believe' it's linked to this one," I say. "I know it is. Now I want to know if you are interrogating me or if you're asking my involvement in the investigation."

"Before we start," Sam cuts in, "were you in the woods earlier?"

Nicolas looks at him strangely.

"In the woods?" he asks. "What do you mean?"

"It's not really an ambiguous question," Sam says, obviously getting the same distasteful vibes off the young officer that I am. "Were you in the woods behind the cabin earlier?"

"No," Nicolas says.

"Then you need to take a note that people are still trespassing. I understand there's probably very little you can do about the house deeper in the woods. But when people are staying in this property, there's a reasonable expectation of privacy and security. Now, I don't purport to know the property lines here in Feathered Nest, but I can imagine the woods within throwing distance of the cabin are the same property. Not long before you got here, there was someone walking right along the edge. Close enough we could hear footsteps from the front porch. As you can imagine, that's not something we particularly want to deal with, considering everything else that's going on," Sam tells him.

It's enough to put Nicolas in his place without being aggressive, and my heart warms. This man just keeps finding new ways to make me fall for him. But that's for another time. Right now, there are other things on my mind.

"I'll make a note of it," Nicolas nods. "If you see or hear anything else suspicious, don't hesitate to call the department. I will be happy to come out and check it out for you."

"Thank you," Sam says.

"Tell me what you found in the initial investigation," I say, taking full advantage of the new, shifted dynamic of the conversation.

"You saw most of it," Nicolas tells me. "The team swept the entire house and the property, but we didn't find anything else."

"That in and of itself is something," I point out. "That crime scene was gruesome. The amount of blood means it would be incredibly difficult to not leave footprints. You found nothing? No fibers or blood drops?"

"We haven't had a full forensic team out. There hasn't been time for that yet. But nothing immediately obvious. It literally looks like whoever did that disappeared into thin air as soon as it was done," Nicolas explains.

"No," I reply firmly. "It's not like they disappeared. They were there. They brutally murdered Marren Purcell as a part of this twisted game I'm in the middle of, and then they left. Which means they left some sign somewhere. There has to be something."

"If there's trace evidence, the forensic team will find it. For now, we have to move forward with the more obvious elements of the scene. Like the note found on the victim's body. I'm sure you're very familiar with its contents," Nicolas says.

We've been talking for less than five minutes, and I've already begun to twitch at his speech patterns and habits. Having him as my filter throughout the entire investigation is going to wear on me, but again, that's exactly what LaRoche wants. I have to keep my head. I can't let it get to me.

"Yes," I confirm. "I read through it several times."

"Can you make any sense of it?" he asks. "The wording is incredibly strange."

"Of course it's strange. It's not meant to be a manifesto. The point is not to say what he did or why. Like I told LaRoche, it's a game. The next piece of a puzzle," I tell him.

"He?" Nicolas asks, clamping down on the one detail he thought might be a slip-up. "Do you have some sort of indication of who it might be?"

"No," I tell him. "But the behaviors are much more consistent with a male. I can't be absolutely positive, of course. But if I had to make a guess, an educated assumption based on my personal experience in the Bureau, I would say this is the work of a man."

"Alright," Nicolas notes, not sounding convinced. "And why would this man kill Marren?"

"I don't know yet. This man has been toying with me, knowing my need to know what happened to my mother."

"What happened to your mother?" he asks.

"She was murdered seventeen years ago. It was never solved, and there are a lot of questions surrounding it," I tell him.

"Emma Griffin," he says, as if the name has just occurred to him. "Your father was Ian Griffin."

"My father *is* Ian Griffin," I correct him.

"He's been missing for years."

"Eleven. Missing, not dead. He disappeared when I was eighteen years old. But for six years before that, it was just the two of us, because of my mother's death. We never knew what happened to her, and I have spent my life dedicated to finding out and to ensuring it never happens to anyone else. Somehow he knows something, and he's using that to drag me through a gauntlet," I say.

"How?" Nicolas asks. "How are the cases linked?"

"On the train, there were notes that led me from one part of the train and one victim to the other. They were all like this. Disconnected, strange, almost like riddles. I had to figure out each little piece in order to move on to the next. At this point, he's escalating. It's hard to imagine escalation from what he did on that train, but writing with the blood on the wall is a major jump."

"She'll be the last," Nicolas insists. "We'll figure it out, and he won't be able to hurt anybody else."

I let out a sigh and swallow down a sudden, painful lump in my throat.

"That's the thing. He might have already," I tell him. "The three victims on the train were already dead before he sent me searching for them, but he made the clues seem like I could stop it. What I was really stopping was the bomb that would have detonated if the train got to the station before Sam and I found it. At this point, I have to work like there is someone else whose life is already hanging in the balance. He keeps daring me to catch him, and that's exactly what I have to do."

"Then we need to focus on this investigation, put everything into it. When the department solves the murder, we catch him," Nicolas says.

"No," I tell him. "It's the other way around. As much as I'd like to think he slipped up and left enough clues at Marren's house for the department to find him, I know he didn't. Three people were murdered, one incapacitated, and another strapped to a bomb on a train, and the detectives managing that case still haven't found any conclusive forensic evidence. No security footage. Nothing. He knows what he's doing. He's not going to slip up. It's too important I keep following him. He knows what I don't, and he's taunting me with it because he has some twisted conclusion in mind.

"He thinks we're in the middle of a giant round of The Game of Life. Well, I went on my education path, I chose my career card, I got in my tiny plastic car, and I'm doing his bidding. I keep playing because I have to. It will hopefully lead me to what happened to my mother. But in the end, the outcome is more straightforward than that. If he wins, more people die. If I win, they don't. It's as simple as that."

Nicolas stares at me for a long, silent stretch, then offers a slow nod.

"So take your turn."

# CHAPTER SIXTEEN

## IAN

SEVENTEEN YEARS AGO...

Ian carefully measured the ingredients, ensuring he got the proper ratio of each. If he was off, even by a little bit, it could end terribly. This wasn't the first time he had to do this. But he hated it. He hated every time he did it, every time he had to watch the effects of it. But it was his only choice. Sometimes it just needed to be done. And this was one of those times.

He'd studied diligently before the first time, and he never let up on his concentration. Everything was measured; everything was double-checked. Triple-checked. He never trusted himself to gauge the proper amounts on his own. This was far too delicate, too precious. Especially now.

When he finished the mixture, he transferred it into a needleless syringe and went into the living room where Emma still slept. She was so peaceful. Ian knew she'd been crying the night before. He felt the heat of her tears soak through his shirt as she rested her head on his shoulder. He wasn't comforting her. She was comforting him. Not even twelve years old, and already she was holding him up.

This wasn't how it was supposed to happen. He didn't want her to sacrifice the innocence of how she saw the world, the tenderness she was entitled to simply by merit of the few years she'd lived. It was his responsibility to be there for her. He was supposed to protect her, and that was more than just keeping her safe from harm. He was her father, and she should know she could trust him, and he would always be there to take care of her.

But he never anticipated this. He'd made those promises to her the moment he found out Mariya was pregnant. Still so many months away from meeting his child, not even knowing if he was to have a son or a daughter. Every night, he waited for his wife to go to sleep, then scooted down on the bed, so his head rested next to her belly. It was just barely round then. Most people looking at her wouldn't even suspect she was pregnant. The new softness was easily covered with clothes, and even when she was wearing tight shirts, she thought showed off her belly, it looked more like she had just indulged in a few extra helpings at Christmas dinner. That wouldn't surprise anybody who knew her. Mariya loved Christmas and loaded the house with traditional Russian foods.

That's how she told him about the baby. She'd been in the kitchen preparing angel wings. Sweet ribbons of pastry fried crisp and sprinkled with powdered sugar akin to the very best part of a funnel cake—the crunchy tips—only so much better. Ian could smell them where he sat in the living room next to the tree. It was already decorated, and he loved to sit in the darkened room and look at the strands of lights nestled in among the branches.

Mariya had come in carrying a huge platter that she placed on the coffee table in front of the couch. He reached for the first angel wing without really paying attention to the platter, but when he went for his second, she pulled the plate away until he looked at it. That's when he noticed the picture in the middle. A fuzzy gray and white image he couldn't really discern. He knew what it was, but not quite what he was looking at. When Mariya finally pointed it out to him, he was so happy he thought he might explode.

A few weeks later, after another ultrasound gave him a clear view of a tiny head and little fingers, he talked to his baby. He promised he would always take care of it. That he would never let anything happen to it. He told it there would be hard times in life, anger, sadness, disappointment, tears. But he would be there through all of it. He would do anything he could to help, to make things better.

When he made those promises, it was with his hand rested on Mariya's belly. He could feel her heartbeat and the rhythm of her breath. She always gave him strength and kept him together. He never realized how much until she wasn't there anymore. He never anticipated he would have to do without it. That he would have to do without her. When he made those promises to his unborn child, he never would have imagined a day would come when he couldn't fulfill them.

But he couldn't. Not right then. Not without her. As much as he wanted to be the one to give Emma strength, Ian had to rely on her. Emma was there for him. She sat with him in silence, crying without speaking. But he couldn't see the tears. There is no sign of them as she lay there sleeping on the couch. He wondered if, in her sleep, she could smell the scent of her mother coming up off the blanket and that's what gave her peace. The smell and warmth would make it feel like Mariya was holding her again. She could hold on to that for a while longer.

Ian took the syringe and carefully tucked the end into the corner of Emma's mouth. She moved only slightly, and he didn't hesitate. If he took too long dispensing the solution into her mouth, it could choke her. He pressed the plunger to release the sedatives, lightly stroking the front of her throat so Emma would swallow. Like he always did, he watched her for the next several minutes. She'd never had an adverse reaction, but he didn't want to risk it.

When he was confident the medication had done its job and settled her even more deeply into sleep, he went about the unpleasant tasks of getting ready to go. It wasn't supposed to be happening this way. They were going to stay for a while this time. He was taking some time off from traveling, and after this last run, Mariya didn't have any planned for the next couple of weeks. They were going to tell Emma Easter morning that they were staying there in Florida for at least a few months.

Now that was gone. It was time to run again.

He packed bags with the speed of someone used to living life like a bullfrog. Hopping from lily pad to lily pad and hoping not to sink. He tossed the bags in the car, shoved pillows and blankets into the back seat, and added as much food as he could stuff into a box and a giant cooler filled with drinks. He took everything he could without going into the back of the house. He couldn't face it. Someone would come and handle the aftermath. They would make it as though nothing had ever happened. Mariya's blood would be rid from the house just as her spirit was.

The last thing Ian put in the car was Emma. Nestling her down into the center back seat, surrounded by pillows and blankets, he protected her eyes and skin with a sheet he pulled down from the windows. Exhaustion would hit him soon. He hadn't slept in almost thirty-six hours, and the emotions he'd gone through left him feeling drained. But he had to go. He had to push for as long as he possibly could. He would get there. Then the work would begin.

There was so much that had to be done. He had people to help him. Flocks that adored Mariya and would do anything they could to help him. Some things needed to be done just because they were what happened after a death. This wasn't a foreign concept to Ian. In his line of work, death wasn't a distant threat or an abstract idea like it was in other types of employment. It was a very real risk that could come to pass without warning. He'd watched it happen more times than he wanted to consider. They always knew that. Ian and Mariya had been planning for the eventuality of their deaths since the day they married. Not that they ever actually thought he'd have to face it.

Now that he was, he had to tie up all the loose ends of her life. Make all those arrangements that seem so simple from a distance but become an impossible web when you're standing in it. Especially since he had to do it twice.

## CHAPTER SEVENTEEN

### NOW

I don't know what it is or how long it's going to last, but Nicolas and I have come to some sort of tenuous agreement. I'm going to take full advantage of it. The less I have to grapple with him, the more mental energy I'll have to concentrate on figuring this out. I take out my phone, setting it on the table so the three of us can see it. I pull up the picture of the note I had Sam snap before turning it over as evidence and swipe my fingers across the screen to zoom in, so it's easier to read.

*You missed the tea party, Emma.*
*It was lovely.*
*Spice tea and cake.*
*The last, but not the first.*
*It's a shame it's still cold.*
*No flowers for the party.*
*But not too much of a loss.*
*I've always thought roses should be read.*
*These remind me of her funeral.*
*Such a simple casket.*
*Is that why it seemed so light?*

*I know.*
*Come find out.*
*Catch me*

"You missed the tea party," I read, tracing my finger across the first line of the note. "Did you find anything that suggested they ate or drank anything? Cups, food, anything?"

Nicolas shakes his head. "There was nothing out of place in the kitchen and nothing on the table or in the living room."

"How about the teapot?" I ask. "Did you check it and make sure there was nothing in it?"

"There was no teapot in the kitchen," Nicolas says.

"Are you sure?" I ask. "Did you look carefully?"

"I mean, we didn't scour the house looking for a teapot. It didn't seem like it meant anything," he says.

"There are teacups on display in the china cabinet," I point out. "Right inside her living room. Why would she have teacups and not a teapot?"

"I don't know," Nicolas admits. "I can have the team look around the house more carefully if you think it might be something."

"That would be good. What about this part? 'The last but not the first'. The first tea party? He's been here before. He didn't choose her and then show up here and murder her. He's interacted with her before," I say.

"So, it's someone from Feathered Nest?" Nicolas asks.

I make an unsure face and shake my head. "I don't think so. I mean, it's possible, but that doesn't fit with all the other pieces. Whoever this is has been trailing me along from place to place to place. If they were just from Feathered Nest, I don't think they would do that. The first piece of engagement I can trace is a bombing in Richmond that happened after I left."

"The one that happened just before Jake Logan's hearing?" he asks.

"Yes. This person was involved in that somehow, but I don't know exactly how."

"What do you mean involved?"

"He sent me a piece of video that was taken by a girl killed in the explosion. The only way it could be accessed was through her personal cloud. The Bureau has been working on tracing the message and figuring out how the cloud was accessed but hasn't been able to pinpoint it," I explain.

"And you think that's the first time he engaged with you? His first… turn?

"I'm not positive, but that's the one we have solid evidence of. I just don't see somebody from Feathered Nest going to that extreme," I say.

"What's that supposed to mean?" he asks. "Are you trying to say something about people from Feathered Nest?"

"Only that there are plenty of other ways somebody from this town could torture me," I point out.

"So, we need to figure out who has been visiting," Sam says.

"When?" Nicolas asks. "It doesn't say anything about any other time this guy was here. Just that it wasn't the first time he had a tea party with Marren."

"Then we cast a wide net. Check in with as many people as possible. Find out if they had friends or family members visiting. See if any of the property owners around here got interest in their houses. We start like dropping a pebble in a pond. The ripples start close, then spread out. Look at the smallest ripples first," Sam tells him.

"Check last summer," I add.

"Why?" Sam asks.

"'No flowers for the party'. They didn't have any for the party because it's too cold. It's too cold right now for her flower vines to be blooming," I say.

"The vines are right outside the house," Sam points out. "Anyone who gets near her house would see them. They're there all year."

"The vines are there," I specify. "But the note specifically mentions the flowers. This guy knows what color Marren's roses are, which means he had to be here while they were blooming. Late spring or summer."

"What I don't understand is why he would go to this much trouble, only to misspell a word," Nicolas says. He points at the screen. "I've always thought roses should be read'. 'Read' instead of 'red'. That seems pretty careless for somebody who goes to this much detail."

"It's not careless," I tell him. "It's intentional. Everything he does is intentional."

"Then what does it mean? Why would he spell it like that?" Nicolas asks.

"I don't know," I admit. "Something to do with reading? But reading what?"

I shake my head slowly, staring at the note, trying to make sense of it. My lips move slowly as I murmur the words over to myself.

"Such a simple casket," Nicolas whispers a second later.

My head snaps to him. "What?"

He points at the phone, running his finger along one of the lines.

"Such a simple casket. When I first read the note, I thought it was talking about Marren. That roses made him think of her funeral like he's fantasizing about it. It's awkward wording, saying it 'reminds' him, but it was the only thing I could think of. But now that I'm looking at it again, I'm noticing these lines. 'Such a simple casket. Is that why it seemed so light?' He's not thinking about a funeral that's coming, he's thinking about one he's already been to."

"My mother's," I say softly.

"Emma, I thought your mother didn't have a funeral," Sam says. "She was cremated."

My mind immediately goes to the urn sitting on my mantle. It's been in every home I've ever lived in, taking up a prominent space so I can always feel like she's with me. No one's ever seen me do it, but there have been times when I've taken the urn down and sat with it, talking as if she was right there. It's comforting in a way and devastating in another.

"She was," I say. "I have her urn. She wasn't scattered or interred anywhere, and there was no memorial service. But remember what

Bellamy found in Florida. That obituary for my mother mentioned a funeral service. Then not-quite-Greg's name in the guest book. Maybe there really was a service. Just with no body."

"No body?" Nicolas asks.

"The date of the funeral listed in the obituary is after my mother was cremated. My father and I weren't even in Florida at the time. If there was a funeral service for her, none of my family was at it, including her," I say. "I would say that would be a hell of a light casket."

"But did she have red roses?" Sam asks.

What he's really asking dawns on me.

"Because if she did, this person was there," I say. "Or at least knows about it."

"Maybe you should call Bellamy," Sam says.

I snatch my phone up and start pacing as I dial her up. My best friend answers on the second ring.

"Are you doing okay?" she asks.

I spoke to her while we were still at Marren's house, waiting for LaRoche to release us from the scene. I filled her in on what was going on and asked her to tell Eric. They've been taking shifts at the hospital with Greg, only leaving him without one of them when it was absolutely necessary. Even then, there is always another guard there to make sure no one gets in the room with Greg.

"As well as can be expected," I tell her. "I need you to do something for me. Go back through everything you got when you were in Florida and send me what you know about the funeral home. If you have a copy of my mother's obituary, that would be really helpful."

"I'll send it to you as soon as I can," she says.

"Thank you, Bells. I really appreciate everything you do for me."

"Of course," she says. "Anything. Always."

As I hang up the phone, my eyes fall on the wooden bookshelves built into the wall. The leather spines look soft and worn. I turn to Nicolas.

"Marren was a teacher, right?" I ask. "I remember her saying something about that when I talked to her."

He nods.

"High school."

"That's right. She taught Jake Logan. Said he was smart and creative," I say. "And such a good boy for driving people home from the tavern at night so they'd be safe."

"That's one way to put it," Sam rolls his eyes.

"Can you get me into her house?" I ask Nicolas.

"Now?" he asks. "The scene is already secure for the night."

"There's something I need to check," I tell him.

"I'll bring you first thing in the morning. I should be getting home anyway. I have a feeling sleep is going to be at a premium for a while."

It's not good enough for me, but I'll have to accept it. He leaves and I go change into pajamas. There's nothing in the house to eat, and the one restaurant in town other than the tavern still open is a pizza shop that doesn't deliver. Sam dutifully calls in our order, kisses me, and heads out to pick it up, leaving me curled up on the couch, staring at my phone, and waiting.

## CHAPTER EIGHTEEN

The edges of the sky are still pink. I can barely feel my hand wrapped around the first cup of coffee brewed at the bakery on Main Street this morning. Moss crunches under my feet as I walk across Marren's front yard. It would look like a Thomas Kinkade painting if it wasn't for the garish bright yellow crime scene tape draped across the front, slicing through the tranquil morning. I shift my weight back and forth on my feet, trying to warm up. This is one of those February mornings where the weather goes back a couple of months, and it feels like the dead of winter rather than the cusp of spring. It's almost like Mother Nature is taunting us. Giving us one last blast of bone-shattering chill before finally thawing out. It's the meteorological opposite of the calm before the storm.

"Have you talked to him yet?" Sam asks, coming toward me with a bag of donuts.

I wasn't interested in any of the muffins or pastries the bakery had on display when we arrived just after the key turned in the door. All that mattered to me was the coffee dripping down from the old-fashioned copper pot on the back counter. No, this was a morning that called for donuts, which meant sending Sam to the tiny shop near the town green to grab a few of the delectable glazed rings I formed an attachment to in the early mornings a year ago.

"I called him. He answered. At least, I think it was him. There weren't really words coming through the other end of the line. More just grumbles and scratchy sounds," I tell him.

"Well, it is barely dawn," he points out.

"Nicolas told me he would bring me inside the house first thing in the morning," I insist.

"I don't think he meant the first thing that the Earth sees in the morning," he says. "More like first thing after he got out of bed and became a functional human."

"I don't have time for that, Sam. He needs to get here. If that means he is only semi-functional, then so be it. All he needs to do is unlock a door."

The lockbox on the front door looks like the police put the cute little house in shackles. It's meant to keep out prying eyes and would-be sensationalist reporters looking to sell grisly shots to tabloids and ghoul sites. And FBI agents who would rather be doing things on their own rather than having the local police force hovering over my every move.

"What exactly are you looking for?" Sam asks.

"A book," I tell him.

"A... book."

"Yes. The note was just like all the other ones, weird riddles and hints, and something that both is and isn't what it seems to be. So, that's what I'm looking for," I say.

A car pulls up to the curb in front of the house, and Nicolas finally climbs out, coming toward me with a distinctly dragging gait.

"I got two hours of sleep," he grumbles as he walks toward me. "Chief called, and I had to go over the initial findings with him. Then my cat threw up."

"He has good taste," I comment.

"The point is, you could have waited a little longer," he says.

"No," I say, stepping up onto the porch beside him. "I couldn't."

Nicolas opens the lock box and takes out the key that opens

Marren's house. He steps inside first, doing a cursory scan, as is the habit of an investigating officer. I can't see him, but I know if I look behind me, Sam is probably doing the same thing. It's not his crime scene, but it's a habit he won't be getting over anytime soon. He could probably die of old age in his late nineties, and his spirit would still come back to glance over the scene and make sure everything was on the up-and-up.

As soon as I get inside, I move across the living room to the china cabinet I noticed the day before. It caught my eye when I walked into the house, but I didn't really process it until later when the officers brought me out of the family room and into the front living room to talk to me. A piece of furniture that reminded me so much of a cabinet in one of the houses we stayed in during my childhood. I don't really have any other specific memories of that house, and the china cabinet doesn't have any significant meaning to me. It's just one of those things that grabs your attention, and it popped back into my head when we were at the cabin reading the note last night.

I stand in front of the glass doors, staring in at the teacups lined neatly on one of the shelves. Below it, just as I thought I would, I see a small stack of very old leather-bound books. Sam comes up beside me, peering in through the doors.

"Did you see the book you were looking for?" he asks.

"Yeah, I do. And somebody else saw it too," I tell him.

"What do you mean?" he asks.

I point in, careful not to touch the glass. Chances are this scene is going to be just like every other one, in there won't be any forensic evidence to be found. But I can't be too careful. Something as simple as touching the door as I point could smear a single fingerprint.

"Marren kept a really nice house. But it seems she wasn't up to dusting inside the china cabinet very often. Look at the top shelves and under the teacups. See the dust?"

"Yes," Sam says.

"Now look at the books. The bottom one in the stock was moved. If you look really closely, you can see where it shifted just enough to move some of the dust so you can see the shelf under it. Somebody has been in there very recently. And I know the reading material they were after. Do you have a pen?" I ask.

He reaches in his pocket and pulls out a black ballpoint pen engraved with his name. I carefully insert it into the keyhole at the front of the cabinet, tilting it up to create pressure.

"Are you trying to pick a lock with my pen?" he asks.

"No, not pick the lock. Most china cabinets like this are never locked. This one is so old it must have been passed down through her family, and most of the time, the keys to old ones like this are forgotten or discarded. It's not worth the hassle of keeping them locked. I don't see a key anywhere around here, which leads me to believe this will work."

Keeping the pressure consistent between my hand and the pen, I guide the door forward. It doesn't cooperate immediately, but after a few tries, it finally shifts out of place and swings open. I use the back of my shoulder to move it the rest of the way open. Without me having to ask him, Sam reaches into his pocket and offers me his handkerchief. I use it to take out the book on the top of the stack and carry it over to the couch.

"What is it?" Nicolas asks.

"The note talks about a tea party and roses. One thing this guy has been doing since the beginning is manipulating things... names, people, objects. It seems to be one thing, but then it turns out to be or mean something else. He used an anagram as his screen name to get the girl who died in the bombing under his control, then to send me messages through her social media. He's chosen victims based on their names because they sound like my mother's. Everything is just slightly off. Which is why I said the word 'read' wasn't a mistake. He was talking about red roses. But he also meant 'read', as in a book."

I turn it to Sam so he can see the cover.

"*Alice in Wonderland,*" he murmurs.

"Arguably the world's most famous and most disastrous tea party. And the Queen of Hearts wanted the roses red."

"That's right," Nicolas says. "They paint them to make her happy."

"Not to make her happy. To keep her from chopping off their heads," I correct.

He draws in a breath, and I look back down at the book in my lap. Turning it over gingerly, aware of how delicate the cover and pages are after having rested on this shelf for so many years, I slowly open my hands, so the pages fall gently open. There tucked in the trough of the pages, nestled among the nonsense words and feverish imagery, are two delicately folded paper roses.

# CHAPTER NINETEEN

## ANSON

ONE YEAR AGO...

She was pretty. Not beautiful, not necessarily anybody who he would ever look twice at. Not if he didn't have a particular reason. But he could understand the attraction. In fact, her not being beautiful might have been part of it. In most situations, it was far easier to draw in the attention and devotion of a woman who was just a shade shy of beautiful. Not completely unattractive. When a woman was distinctly unattractive or perceived herself to be, she tended to be defensive and more likely to be suspicious of a man engaging with her. Whether that was fair or not, it was an experience he'd had.

Which is why Anson understood as soon as he saw Sarah Mueller from across the visitation room. For the last several months, he'd been reading the letters she sent to Travis Burke. They were written in code. At least, what she thought was code. It was more just a juvenile jumble of letters and words anyone who paid attention could see through. But he didn't let on that he knew that. He was just as enraptured by her as she was by Travis. That was the beginning. He had already gained Travis's trust. And now he needed to gain Sarah's.

Meeting Travis was nothing short of serendipity. Anson didn't intentionally search him out or do anything to make his way into the prison where the murderer was serving his time. He was there to visit Craig, a member of Leviathan who'd offered himself up as a sacrificial lamb when the police had come too close to unraveling one of the events of chaos they planned. That didn't happen often. Usually, Leviathan's plans were so meticulous, and so carefully executed, investigations rarely went far. That was part of the fun. The police, and even the FBI, knew someone was responsible for what was happening, but they couldn't get even close to narrowing down who.

That's not how it worked out that time. The release of nitrogen gas into a large sightseeing elevator system was glorious. The glass elevator hung high above the ground, stopped so no one could get out, and everyone on the street below could watch the panic unfolding above their heads. With nothing to conceal the people inside, those so shocked they couldn't look away simply watched in horror as the gas stole the oxygen in the tight glass capsules. There was no color and no smell, nothing to alert the people inside that something was wrong. And because the elevators weren't airtight to the point of a complete seal, there was just enough of a slow drip of oxygen coming in from outside to dilute the effect of the nitrogen for a few extra seconds. The gas affected people at different times. It all depended on the rate of respiration, overall health, age, size. All those factors that could be so random in a crowd and make chaos all the more prevalent.

The body interprets nitrogen as oxygen, thinking it's breathing exactly what it's supposed to. But it doesn't take long for reality to set in. It's not like carbon monoxide, which puts a person to sleep before slowly killing them. With nitrogen, the body just keeps going until it can't anymore. Death is usually silent and extremely sudden. Some may pass out first but will die very shortly thereafter. Others will be going about whatever they're doing and suddenly collapse dead.

Different rates of reaction meant a few of the large group in the elevator fell to the floor, dead at the feet of the other people, who immediately began to panic. That panic only increased the rate of breathing, which drew more of the nitrogen gas into their bodies so soon others fell. This led to a few magnificent moments of watching them crawl over each other and claw at the glass walls, screaming in desperation, while no one underneath could hear. Fire engines screamed for them and raced to the building to try to open the elevator. One by one, the tourists dropped as the firefighters did everything they could to get to them. They eventually pried the doors open, and the rush of fresh air saved the few still lingering.

It had been incredible to watch, but there was a minor flaw in the planning and execution. It meant too many detectives sniffing around and drawing close to the organization. They couldn't risk that. Leviathan couldn't risk any chance that the outside world—especially the authorities—would learn not only of their existence but of their mission. So they did what had to be done. Every member of Leviathan knew there could come a day when they would be called upon to give themselves up for the good of the organization. Allowing themselves to be arrested and convicted of crimes associated with the events of chaos preserved the sanctity of the rest. Within the organization, they were seen as martyrs, honored, and respected.

That made the time they had to spend in prison far more comfortable than it was for virtually any of the other prisoners. Members of their ranks wielded power in various spheres of public life, who could grease the wheels for the captured member to serve their time in the prison ideal for them. That might mean a prison close to family, medium-security rather than maximum, or a facility with the kinds of features and programs they want the most. They thought of it as being caught in a net, trapped for the amusement of others because they swam in the wrong waters.

But being kept in a tank didn't mean they couldn't be well-cared-for. Lotan provided a constant stream of funds, and other members visited frequently. It wasn't unheard of for contraband and untraceable bribes from the outside to ensure the prisoner perks not available to anyone else. They could even gain favor with the guards and other staff, affording themselves even greater access and privilege. It would be better for them to be free, but when that wasn't an option, the organization didn't turn their back.

Unless, of course, the captured one was disposable. Bait. Then they were fed into the system and quickly turned into a commodity or a casualty. Depending on the situation, it was sometimes hard to know which would be better.

That wasn't the case with Craig. He gave himself up and garnered the masterful skill of several powerful attorneys secretly associated with Leviathan. They crafted a defense so intricate and compelling it managed to create sympathy. Not an easy task for someone charged with terrorism, the public murders of ten people and attempted murder of several more. But the decimation of the criminal justice system prevailed, and he was set in the lap of comparative luxury. Anson became one of his most frequent visitors. And there he learned about Travis.

One of the greatest benefits of having one of their own caught in a net and kept in the tank was they were now among others who held a certain power and influence. While many of those rotting away in prison cells could do little if anything for the mission of Leviathan, others were valuable sources of information, networking, and control. Craig had only been inside for a few weeks when he met Travis Burke. The younger man had recently been transferred from another facility, and the story of his crime had rustled through general population. He'd been convicted of brutally murdering his wife, burying her in a cement case, then digging her up and moving her, all the while pretending to be the desperate husband searching for the lost woman he loved.

It wasn't a new story. That happened fairly frequently. It was actually astonishing when Anson thought about it. No matter how frequently it didn't work, people still seemed to believe they could kill someone and get away with it just by saying that person walked away from their life. Usually, it took a matter of days to find all the loose threads that led directly to the murder. It was a catastrophe of bad planning. But not for Travis. He managed to keep up the ruse for quite some time. That is until a brand-new FBI agent came onto the scene and quickly unraveled him: Emma Griffin.

Anson, of course, already knew that name. He'd known it for many years and had grown to hate it. That wasn't the way it was at first. He admired her—at least the idea of her—as much as anyone else in the organization. He could see how much she meant to Lotan and understood his longing for her. She was taken from him, and it twisted and disturbed his mind. Anson felt for the leader he was so devoted to. But over time, that faded. He no longer saw Emma Griffin as a tragic figure. She was no more than the green light at the end of Daisy's Pier. And like Gatsby, Lotan was letting himself spiral away into nothingness because of her. He'd lost his commitment to the mission. Time that should have been spent planning events and orchestrating the trades and sales that had built up his power and wealth was frittered away on following her movements, tracing her, and waiting for the perfect moment.

But that moment would never come. He didn't see that, but Anson did. Lotan wanted everything to be perfect for Emma to give her the life he'd never been able to because the opportunity was robbed from him. It was a delicate process; he would tell those closest to him. It was a careful strategy to ensure she wasn't damaged and instead could welcome him into her life with open arms.

It was a mistake for Lotan to entrust Anson with his inner thoughts. To share the way he felt about Emma with him. It wasn't out of affection. He shared because he needed Anson to do things for him, to make sure plans fell into place outside the bubble he created around Emma, so he could concentrate more on her. And he started to stumble. Lotan served time when none could save him. He lost track of Emma and became even more desperate. And when he found her again, it was all his mind could focus on.

And Anson became bitter. This woman had destroyed what he held most sacred, what he believed in more than anything in the world. She wasn't even worth it. There was nothing about her that was special or impressive, nothing valuable or exceptional. And he would prove it.

Sarah Mueller was going to help him.

## CHAPTER TWENTY

### GREG

A YEAR AND A HALF AGO...

The change happened so quickly, that when it was finally done and reality sank in, Greg questioned if what he thought happened actually did. From the very beginning, he'd thought he understood what was happening. He knew what he signed himself up for. He had always been willing to take great personal risk in the name of preserving freedom and safety. This was at his core why he had joined the FBI, to begin with. He wanted to do anything he could to protect people and to make the world a slightly safer place to be. That seemed like such a cliché now. How could he possibly have had that dream when he didn't even know what the world is actually like?

What he saw in those dark nights wasn't like anything he had ever seen or imagined. He knew horror. He knew of cruelty and war. But the joy they found in the depravity and the way they justified it made what he saw Lotan and Fisher do more disturbing than any of it.

Things had started so well. They were exactly what he thought they were going to be, and he'd committed himself wholly to the project. There were days when he longed for his old life and missed people. Especially Emma. But he'd told himself he couldn't think that way. He couldn't be so selfish as to want to return to that normalcy when there was so much good he could be doing here. Emma would understand. The day would come when he would be able to stand in front of her proudly and tell her everything he'd accomplished. Lotan had already promised him. Greg would be the one to return her to her beloved father.

He couldn't wait for that moment. He'd often gone to sleep with that thought painting crisp images on the backs of his eyelids. It would be such an incredible moment. One of such relief and happiness for her. And if he was going to make sure that happened, he had to do everything that was asked of him. He had to give of himself completely and in every way possible to make sure the assignment was completed.

Those thoughts dissolved away quickly. Soon he began to realize what was being asked of him benefited no one but the man they called Lotan. He'd come to despise hearing that name. This man didn't deserve a title of respect, a name that would mean anything. He was Ian Griffin, the CIA agent of legend; a man people still spoke of in hushed tones because of the incredible legacy he left when he disappeared. But Greg didn't even think he deserved to be called that.

Everybody always wondered what had become of Ian. His disappearance was orchestrated, that was obvious. He didn't just walk away without any preparation or planning, and he wasn't taken. He had gone through a tremendous amount of effort to make sure everything was in place before he left. It couldn't have been easy for him to leave Emma. At least Greg knew she was a grown woman who had been standing on her own two feet for many years and would be fine without him if she had to be. But when her father left, Emma was barely an adult. She had only just turned eighteen and was looking ahead to her entire life. Granted, she was probably better prepared than most people who reach that age, but it still couldn't have been easy for her. It was reassuring and comforting to Greg that he hadn't put her in that same position.

But the thoughts always lingered. The questions of what could have possibly justified him leaving her life like that, never to hear from him for so many years. Though he obviously didn't know about it at the time it happened, when Greg found out the story of Emma's father, he could see why it would be everybody's first assumption he had gone off on an undercover mission. Especially if it was going to be in a particularly dangerous location, or if his goals were treacherous, he would want to put preparations in place to ensure his child was going to be well taken care of. Then he just didn't come back. He didn't reach out to anyone. He didn't give any indication to anyone he was alive and well. Or even just alive.

And no one knew anything. The CIA came forward stating they weren't aware of any assignments, and they had him officially listed as missing. Of course, Ian had an explanation for that. His mission, what they had to do, was so confidential, so incredibly classified, everybody was in on it. The entire government was working together to conceal his identity and protect him while he did what needed to be done. And Greg believed him. He believed every word he said to him, and the more he thought about it as the days slipped by, the sicker it made him feel.

Then everything changed. It had already been slowly crumbling away, falling between his fingers and dissolving into ash in front of his face. But he had to face what was actually happening. After all the deaths. After the blood. After watching the man he respected so much hand over weapons to cartels and accept drugs, he would then sell for even greater profit. Or save, to brandish around and keep people quiet. Other Leviathan operatives didn't get to use it, Greg learned after the second transaction like that he witnessed. The first one he thought was being done to collect intelligence, the beginning of infiltration. The second one he knew was purely for profit.

That's when he learned the drugs weren't for entertainment or solace. Lotan wasn't going to dole them out as an extra perk to those who were loyal to him. Instead, they became a method of torture and eventual execution. Greg would never forget the sounds of the men forced into addiction, then put in an empty room and left to go through withdrawal, only to be injected again just as it was over so the spiral could begin again. For some of these men, their agony would eventually atone for whatever mistake they'd made, and they would be released after their final withdrawal.

But for others, the torment would end with an overdose. They'd be callously tossed out into the street or the landfill, where they'd be seen as another statistic, another disgusting addict not worth the time or energy to investigate.

By then, Greg came to know that this man wasn't what people thought he was. It wasn't until a simple slip that Greg found out he wasn't who Greg thought he was, either.

"How can you spend so much time at a place like that?" Greg asked Fisher when he returned from visiting one of the prisons.

That was part of Fisher's role within the organization. He took care of the ones in the tank. But Greg couldn't understand why the man always returned seeming happy, rather than dragged down by the sheer reality of the place.

"What do you mean?" Fisher asked. "A prison?"

"Yes," Greg nodded. "If I had to spend as much time visiting inmates at prisons and jails as you do, I'd be miserable."

"Why?"

Greg was shocked by the question and not really sure how to answer. It seemed obvious.

"The people," Greg said. "Those places are literally warehouses full of degenerates and criminals."

He stopped himself short of pointing out both Fisher and their fearless leader deserved to be among those ranks. Fisher still looked at him like he couldn't comprehend what he was saying.

"You use the word 'warehouse,'" he said. "I thought people who worked in law enforcement were supposed to have more respect for the criminal justice system than that. You're supposed to see prisons and jails as rehabilitation centers and places where the good within can thrive," he said sarcastically. "But even you can admit that most of the time, they're just places to toss the people society has gotten tired of or who they can't handle anymore."

"Or the ones who don't deserve to be a part of society anymore," Greg pointed out.

"And who are you to determine that?" Fisher said. "Who gets to decide what's right for society?"

"Like you said. The criminal justice system," he answered.

"The criminal justice system is corrupt and broken. It keeps people oppressed and afraid rather than alive. We are working toward revolution. Chaos is life. It's freedom. People who go every day the exact same as they did the day before, with nothing to change them, nothing to make them think or act, aren't living. People are being persecuted and put in cages for pursuing happiness and keeping others feeling alive," Thomas Fisher told him.

"And destroying and killing others," Greg replied.

"Not everyone gets to the promised land. Even Moses was stopped before he made it in, and he was the one leading the pack. Sometimes it just doesn't work out the way people want it to. You want to think the ones who follow the rules should get power and control in return. But Lotan gained some of his most powerful connections and learned his most valuable lessons when he was in prison."

That stopped Greg like a jolt to his chest.

"Lotan went to prison?" Greg asked

Fisher scoffed. "Yes. Those were better times. He was still strong, still focused. He hadn't become so obsessed with Emma Griffin that he forgot his way."

Greg's eyes grew wide, and Fisher gave a mirthless laugh.

"You think everyone is as a slovenly devoted to him as you are, don't you? I've learned to play this game over the years. I've watched Lotan shrink away from being a force of nature that could craft and destroy with a snap of his fingers, to a mere man desperate for the attention of a woman people worship for reasons I can't even come close to comprehending."

He gave Greg a simpering look. "Oh. I'm sorry. You love her, don't you? Then maybe you can tell me why she's so important. Why he has completely lost himself over her and his obsession with finding the right moment to tell her the truth."

Greg forced himself to stay calm, to maintain his control. He didn't want to let on to the doubts going through his head or the emotions starting to surge through him.

"When was he in prison?" he asked.

"Fifteen years ago," he says. "For five years."

"Does he have any idea how you feel about him?" Greg asked, inching closer to the line, but staying steady.

"No. And you're not going to tell him. Because the thing is, if you did, you know how it would work out. First, he wouldn't believe you. Why would he? I do everything he asks. Second, you want to see the light of day again. And you know if you say anything to him about me, you never will." Fisher's eyes traveled up and down Greg briefly. "Your chances are slim as it is. You're losing your value."

As he walked away, Greg knew he'd lost far more than that. He'd heard everything he needed to. Fifteen years before, Emma was a young teenager whose mother was already dead. And whose father, Ian Griffin, never left her for more than a week after drastically cutting back on his travel for work.

Not caring about Fisher's warning, Greg went directly to Lotan. He wouldn't say anything about the other man's disdain. That was between Fisher and Lotan. It wasn't in his nature to speak for other people or spread rumors. But he would speak for himself.

"Hello, Lamb," he said, sounding both surprised and put off by his appearance. Up until now, Greg had been one of the honored few still allowed to look directly at Lotan and speak. He had a feeling that wasn't going to last much longer. "What can I do for you?"

"Who are you?" he asked.

A smile wound its way onto Lotan's face, and he reached in front of him to slip the pen he was using back into the penholder at the front edge of his desk.

"What do you mean? You know who I am," he replied.

"No," Greg shook his head. "Who are you? Because you aren't Ian Griffin. You aren't Emma's father."

Lotan's fingers folded over each other as he rested them on his desk.

"Well, those are two different things, aren't they?" He tilted his head slightly to the side like he was considering Greg, waiting for a response. When it didn't come, he straightened it again.

"No. I'm not Ian Griffin. But I am Emma's father. She just doesn't know it yet."

## CHAPTER TWENTY-ONE

NOW

Sam slides the rest of the book into his lap as I take out the paper roses and look at them from all angles. They've been flattened by the book but are painstakingly folded to resemble roses in full bloom. The outside of the pedals have a thin wash of red paint, but I can see words on the insides. I tilt one of the roses so Sam and Nicolas can see the words inside.

"The roses should be read," I say.

Unfolding the first rose, I spread the page out on the arm of the sofa beside me. It looks like a page of text from the book, but the longer I look at it, the more I realize it's far bigger than the scale of the antique and seems to have been printed on conventional paper rather than the thicker cardstock of classic books. But what really stands out to me is the vibrant yellow highlighter splashed across the page.

"Alice," Sam murmurs.

I nod. "Every time the name Alice appears on the page, it's highlighted."

Nicolas reaches for the paper, and I hand it over to him. His eyes scan over the words, taking in how many times the bright yellow ink boxes in the titular character's name.

"Do you know someone named Alice?" he asks. "Is this another clue?"

"I don't know anybody named Alice," I say. "Not anybody that I can think of, anyway. Sam?"

He shakes his head.

"No." Then something seems to occur to him. "Alice Brooks."

"Alice Brooks?" Nicolas frowns. "Who is that? Could she be in danger?"

I let out a breath, feeling the tips of my fingers start to tremble just with the mention of her name.

"She isn't in any danger," I say. "She's already dead."

"Dead?" he asks.

"It's not recent. She died last year. It was the first case Sam and I investigated together." I shake my head. "But I don't think this is about her. I don't think it's going to have anything to do with her."

"It's happened before," Sam points out.

"I know. But Sarah's gone. This isn't about our old cases. I know it's the same name, but I really don't think it could have anything to do with her. There has to be another explanation."

"Who's Sarah?" Nicolas asks.

I'm remembering even more clearly now why I didn't want to have to shadow him this investigation. His questions are already grating on me, and I don't want to have to give them the blow-by-blow of everything just to get the access I need.

"She was linked to the first case I had with the Bureau," I explained. "She was angry about me putting her boyfriend in prison and came back to torment me. Eventually, she took pieces of my old cases and recreated them out of some psychotic obsession with me. But that's not important right now. She's dead. She has been for months. The name is a coincidence. It has to be."

"Then what does it mean? He went to all this trouble to get you to a copy of Alice in Wonderland so he could bring your attention to the name Alice. But why?" Sam asks.

"I don't know," I admit. "But we have another rose."

I open it, expecting another page from the book, or possibly a page from a different one. Instead, the paper is almost blank. The words visible from the inside of the petals cover a small portion of the top of the page.

"What is that?" Nicolas asks.

I bring the paper closer, so I can see it more carefully. It doesn't look like the words were typed directly onto the page. Instead, it's as if another piece of paper was layered on top of something and scanned.

"It looks like a medical record," Sam notes. "Or at least, part of one."

"That's exactly what it is," I nod, not sure if my voice is even loud enough to hear over the breath escaping my lungs.

"Whose is it?" Nicolas asks. "Alice's?"

"No," I say. "It's my mother's."

Sam takes the page from my hand and reads the information.

"This is definitely your mother's name," he says. "Mariya Presnyakov."

"It's also her birthdate," I point out.

"This says it's for a hospital in Rolling View," Sam says.

"That's not far from here," Nicolas tells us. "Maybe twenty minutes."

"Why would my mother be at a hospital twenty minutes from here?" I ask.

Taking the page out of his hand, I read over the words again. All of it is right there, her name, her birth date, height, and weight that sound like an accurate description of how I remember her. But very little else.

"It says the doctor she saw was M. Morrison. Does that sound familiar?" Sam asks.

"No," I shake my head. "None of this does. It doesn't make any sense. Look at the date. August 1990. That's the year before I was born. But neither of them ever mentioned being anywhere near here to me. And they told me about all of their adventures. They didn't move around nearly as much before I was born. And according to the papers we got from Iowa, they still lived there in 1990. My grandparents still owned the house there and hadn't moved to Sherwood yet. It's entirely possible they were traveling at the time, but where would they vacation anywhere around here? And even if they were, why would she end up in a hospital because of it?"

"And this isn't an emergency," Sam points out. "If something happened while she was traveling, she got hurt or sick or something; she would go to the emergency room or an urgent care center. This looks like an official medical record, like part of one for a consistent patient."

"So, my mother had a doctor halfway across the country? That doesn't seem terribly convenient."

"Is that it?" Nicolas asks. "That's all that's here?"

"That's it," I tell him.

"It's something," Sam offers. "Now we figure out where to go from here."

"The forensic team still hasn't come in," Nicolas reminds me.

I let out a sigh. "So, I can't look anywhere else, or I might alter the evidence. That isn't there. Because he doesn't leave evidence."

"I want to talk to the neighbors. See what they know. I'm sure they've already been interviewed, but maybe they'll remember something else or be more forthcoming when it's not someone in uniform. It's still too early for that, though. I'm going to go back to the cabin and do some research. I want to get in touch with the hospital and request my mother's medical records. Hopefully, they won't be difficult about it and require me to petition the courts for them," I say.

"Why would that happen? You're her daughter and she's..."

"Dead? I know. But HIPPA laws aren't. Technically her dying doesn't release the records to the estate. They are still the private information of the dead person and the property of the facility. The legal representative of that person can request them, but because I was not quite twelve when she died, that's not me. It's my father. For obvious reasons, I can't ask him to request the file, which puts me at the mercy of the hospital itself. If the administration is understanding, they will let me have them. If not, my only chances will be to petition for them."

Nicolas stares back at me.

"Okay," he says flatly. "I guess if you're going to do that, I'm going to go to the station and try to grab some sleep on the cot. That way at least I'm already there when LaRoche starts calling."

"I'll let you know if I need anything else from you," I say.

We start toward the door, and he stops, turning back to face me.

"Griffin," he says. "Don't come back here without me. Don't try to get inside or search anything. Understand?"

I draw back my shoulders, letting out a stream of breath to calm myself, then give a single nod.

"Yes," I tell him.

He opens the door and waves us through before closing it and securing the lock and lockbox again. Sam and I climb into the car, and he looks down at the book in my hands. I've pressed the roses back in place to protect them.

"You probably should have given him those for evidence," he points out.

"He didn't ask for them," I point out. "This means nothing to any of them. It won't help with their investigation. I just want them for a little while; then I'll turn them in."

"Fine," he relents. "Do you want to stop at the store on the way back to the cabin?"

"Sure," I tell him. "We need stuff in the kitchen. It should be open by now."

We're not even the first customers through the door. The sun is fully up, and Feathered Nest is awake. Most of the groceries we choose are for me since Sam has to go back to Sherwood tomorrow. I don't want to think about that right now. Piling everything into the backseat, we head back to the cabin as the sunlight outside begins to look like a warm day. Some sleepiness has started to settle in when we get to the door, but it disappears as soon as we open it.

The loud, piercing sound coming from the inside of the cabin is unmistakable. I run into the kitchen and stop so suddenly Sam stumbles into my back and has to wrap an arm around my waist to steady us both. I swallow hard, my eyes locked on the stove.

"I think we found Marren's teapot."

## CHAPTER TWENTY-TWO

As Sam walks into the living room to make a phone call, I notice something hanging from the edge of the teapot. I look more closely and realize it's the tags of teabags submerged in the water inside and held in place by the lid. Were it not for some person—undoubtedly Catch Me—breaking into my house, it would be a nice touch, actually brewing the tea as it heats up. I'm about to turn around and join Sam when the words written on the tags catch my eye. Picking them up, I read each of the three. They're all identical.

"He's on his way," Sam says, coming back in the room. "He said he should be here in just a minute. Emma? Is something wrong?"

"The tea," I say. "Look at the type of tea that's brewing." He comes to stand beside me, and I show him the tags. "It's supposed to be holiday spice. You can smell it. It smells like cinnamon and nutmeg. But the word holiday is blacked out. So they just say spice."

"Spice tea," he sighs. "Where's the cake?"

"Do you think it has to do with Sarah's cake she baked for me?"

"Spice," Sam frowns. "Why does that ring a bell in my head? Other than, you know, cooking spices."

"I don't—" I start to say, but then it floods back into me. "Spice.

Spice Enya? That company Bellamy found out about in Iowa. Spice tea on the note. And come to think of it, remember a couple of weeks ago we got that flyer on the door to 'Spice Up Your Life'?"

"I thought that was just for a dance class."

"I did too. But no other house on the street had that flyer. That's too many coincidences with that word."

"Why does that word keep following you?"

"It means something. It has to. Bellamy was never able to find out any more about the company Spice Enya that supposedly bought the house in Iowa. Nothing. There's no information for it at all. But it has to mean something."

We walk out onto the porch to wait for Nicolas, standing close together in front of the door that was purposely left partially cracked. Neither one of us want to admit how unnerving finding the teapot is. I'd rather just say we are standing so close because of the cold. Nicolas must have been driving down Main Street, probably looking for somewhere to pick up breakfast before going into the station because it doesn't take him too long to get to the cabin. He moves quickly to us as soon as he gets out of the car, his hand noticeably rested on the gun at his hip.

"Where was it?" he asks.

"On the stove," I tell him. "Come in; I'll show you."

We cross through the cabin into the kitchen and stand at the side of the stove, staring at the gradually cooling teapot.

"And it was like this when you came in?" he asks.

"No. It was on the burner and whistling. Somebody took the time to not only bring it here, but to fill it with water and tea, and set it to boil. It was whistling full blast when we got here, so it had been long enough for the water to reach a full boil. But there's still plenty in the pot. It hasn't evaporated away yet, so it wasn't on here for too long. It's not a very big window."

"I'll call for backup, and we'll search the area. I'm sure you had the door locked, right?" he asks.

"Of course we did," I say. "I already told you we had somebody creeping around here last night before you got here. I'm not going to just leave the door open and invite everybody in."

"Look around. See if anything has been taken or moved. I'm going to call the station."

He walks outside to use the radio in his car to get backup, and Sam and I start searching the cabin. Just like last night, there doesn't seem to be anything different about it than it was when we left early this morning. Everything is in the same place, and I don't notice anything new. We go through each of the rooms carefully; then I bring him over to the basement door.

"Not my favorite place in the cabin," I say, remembering the moment the electricity went out, and Jake easily navigated down to the circuit breaker, confirming my suspicions about him.

"Do you want me to check it out?" he asks.

I shake my head. "I'll be fine."

We go down into the basement and look around. There's very little in the tight space, so it doesn't take long to confirm there's no one hunkered down here waiting to jump out at us. As we climb back up onto the main floor, Nicolas comes back into the cabin.

"They'll be here soon. Did you notice anything missing or changed?" he asks.

"No. Everything's exactly like it was before we left except for the lovely spot of tea the cabin apparently prepared for us by itself," I say. "Holiday Spice."

"That's a bit out of season."

"It also wasn't in the cabin. It was intentional. The word 'holiday' is blacked out," I say.

"So, just 'spice'?" he asks.

"The word 'spice' has been following me around since I started finding out more about my family's past. There's a company called Spice Enya that owns the house my grandparents used to and where my family lived for a while, but we haven't been able to find out anything about the company. There have been a few times now where I've encountered it," I tell him.

"That's a strange company name," he notes. "Especially for investment."

"It is," I confirm. "But obviously it means something."

The young officer glances to the side just slightly, like he's trying to see a fleeting thought that's getting away from him. It only lasts a second before he looks back at me again.

"We're going to want to search ourselves if that's alright with you."

"That's fine. I'm not going to be here," I say.

"What do you mean?" Sam asks.

"You do realize this means Catch Me is here. In Feathered Nest. He knew when we left, and he knew when we were on our way back. I don't know about you, but I don't exactly feel like sitting around here today. Start calling the hotels around here."

I head for the door and Sam follows.

"You want to find somewhere else to stay?" he asks.

"No. I want to find out who else is staying around here."

I'm already on the phone with the nearest hotel by the time I climb into the car.

"My name is Agent Griffin. I'm with the FBI," I say as the clerk answers at the first hotel.

"What can I help you with?" she asks.

"Can you tell me how many people have checked in over the last five days?"

"Give me just a minute."

I wait impatiently until she comes back and gives me a rundown of everybody who has checked in to the hotel. She's able to give me a few details about them, and the fact that most of them have already checked out. None of them sound like the right person, though, and I thank her before hanging up. I'm about to look up the number to the next hotel when a thought flashes through my mind. Sam gets behind the wheel as I'm calling Nicolas.

"Are you still outside?" he asks.

"Yes, but we're leaving. I need you to do something for me. Have somebody from the station get in touch with every hotel within a twenty-mile radius. Have them print out the information for everyone who has checked in for the last week. Actually, make that two weeks. Most of them will probably be fine handing it over to the police, but if they put up a fight because there's no warrant, start working on one. If this guy got a room to stay in while he's here playing tag with me, we need to find him," I say.

"Anything else?" he asks, some of the aggravation returning to his voice.

"Yes. Have people out in the woods, campgrounds, empty buildings. Check for any signs of camping," I say. "And lock up when you leave."

"Why are you having them get the hotel information?" Sam asks when I get off the phone. "I thought that's what you were doing."

"It was, but I changed my mind. There's a specific one I want to go to," I explain.

"Why?"

"The note left on the car said 'Jake gives his regards'. In any other situation, I might say it was just a disturbing touch for the sake of being disturbing. But not with this guy. He doesn't do anything without a meaning. So, maybe it's time to go back to the beginning of the investigation."

"Wouldn't that be the cabin?"

"The investigation into Ron Murdock."

# CHAPTER TWENTY-THREE

## LOTAN

FIFTEEN YEARS AGO...

"Don't let the sun catch you crying," he sang softly to himself as he walked down the dusty hallway.

Hours had passed since he'd first climbed into the hotel and waited. He didn't realize how much time had passed. That old saying must really be right. Time flies when you're having fun. Only, he wouldn't really say this was fun. Satisfying and vindicating, yes. But every moment was reliving the pain of that night two years before, when he'd discovered the only woman he ever loved was taken from the planet. And he couldn't forget the day it was. Seeking vengeance was in honor of Emma's birthday, but he couldn't bring himself to feel celebratory. Not yet. Maybe the day would come that he would be able to have those feelings.

That day would come. He couldn't let himself think otherwise. As much as it hurt to be away from her now, it wouldn't always be this way. When this night was done and he had fulfilled the duties he placed on himself, he would have to take a step back for a while. But when that time was done, all his concentration could go back to Emma. He would find her and take her back. That would take time.

He knew that. It wasn't going to be as simple as walking into her life and having her know immediately who he was. Lotan wished that could happen. It would be his greatest joy. The greatest joy he was capable of now, anyway. But that wasn't realistic.

She already had a lifetime of programming and carefully told lies creating the construct of her life. Everything Emma believed and felt was because that's what was taught to her. She couldn't help it. She was still so young and impressionable. Especially now after losing her mother. She would cling desperately to what she thought she knew, and it would be traumatic for her to face another sudden change. That's why he had to be patient and take his time. But it would be worth it. He had already waited this long for her. Waiting a little longer was a small sacrifice.

Ahead of him, one of the boards covering up a window had slipped just enough to let in a bit of light from outside. It wasn't quite sunrise yet. Just that hazy part of night that comes just after the darkest moments. When moonlight and starlight start to blend together, and the edges of the world begin to glow. It was the sight of that light when he was walking away from the pool that got the old British Invasion songs stuck in his head. He hummed one now as he continued walking down the hallway. It was quiet, but that didn't discourage him.

Levi must not have realized how much dust was on the floor. The freshest footsteps were easy to discern from the older ones already covering over with new particles drifting down from the ceiling. Some footprints even overlapped in differing levels of dust, where each of the three men had passed over the same place several times. But Lotan could still identify them. He could tell which of the footprints were different from those leading to the door to the roof. Boots for him, flimsy broken down sneakers for Thomas.

Tracing the footsteps with the beam of his flashlight and the helpful glow coming in from around the hotel, he could make a guess where Levi had gone. It was one of those choices that might seem obvious, the best place to go if he couldn't get out of the hotel but needed to not be so visible. But in reality, it was a terrible choice. The echoing of the heavy door leading down to the mostly empty basement meant there were few places to hide.

Lotan's humming got louder as he walked slowly down the stairs, letting each of his footfalls accent the song. Down here was still completely dark. There were no windows to let in the faint beginning of light, and the emergency bulbs that would have once glowed in the upper corners of the ceiling had long since extinguished. It was dark, but the basement wasn't completely quiet. To one side, he heard squeaks and the faint scratching of tiny claws. He smiled. Now he knew both of his traps had worked. Humans in one. Rats in the other.

He swept his light around the room, catching every corner and bending around stacks of old furniture and boxes that looked like they were filled with unclaimed possessions from previous guests. It didn't take long for him to hear choked, terrified breathing. As hard as Levi was trying to control himself and stay silent enough to escape, he couldn't. The terror had taken over. And for good reason.

Lotan steadied himself. He dried his hands of as much of the blood as possible so he wouldn't lose grip on his chain. As he pulled it out of his bag, Levi burst out from behind a stack of boxes. He rammed into Lotan, knocking him backwards, so his flashlight skidded across the floor. Lotan hit the ground but was back up on his feet in an instant. He could hear Levi running, and he snatched his flashlight to find him.

It was obvious the other man was disoriented and turned around because instead of heading toward the exit, he was moving deeper into the basement. Lotan didn't mind. The maze wasn't complicated. There wasn't enough still stored down here to create many places to cower. But it was still a touch more excitement. Let Levi run and dart for a few moments before he tired of the chase. Following the echo of his footsteps, Lotan looped around, so Levi had no choice but to run directly toward him. One hard hit on the side of the head with the flashlight rendered him dizzy and unstable on his feet. He tried to keep going, but Lotan wrapped the length of chain around both of his hands and swept it around Levi's head, whipping him around in one movement, so he stood behind him with the chain twisted tight.

Levi gasped and struggled against the chain. He tried to kick Lotan, to force him away. But he'd been through so much over the last two years. His body wasn't strong and resilient like it used to be. It almost seemed relieved to be giving up and sinking down under the crushing pressure of the chain on the front of his throat, though his eyes were still wide in terror as Lotan brought him to the floor and rolled him over.

He clawed at the floor in much the same way that Thomas had clawed at the roof, trying to drag himself away from Lotan.

"Where are you trying to go, Levi?" he asked. "Do you think you can just escape?"

Lotan yanked the chain. It cut deeper into the man's neck. Levi tried to say something, but his voice wouldn't come out.

"I'm sorry," Lotan said calmly. "I can't hear you. You'll really have to speak up next time. It's been lovely seeing the two of you again, but I really must be going now. You understand. There's just one thing I need to do first."

He stepped over Levi and used the chain to drag him across the floor. Levi kicked and thrashed as hard as he could, but his strength was waning quickly. Lotan got to the wooden box he had already prepared. Before luring the men here by pretending to be another defector from Leviathan wanting to help them, he'd spent time in the hotel, getting familiar with it and preparing what he needed. It was easy to secure the room doors that weren't already locked, so they had fewer places to go. He had no trouble getting accustomed to the hallways and the sounds of the different areas. By now, he could navigate it even without being able to see clearly.

But this box had been more of a challenge. It needed to be perfect. Thomas had torn away his heart, so Lotan tore away his life. Levi had trapped him in a suffocating place impossible to escape from while the agony of losing Mariya ate away at him. So he would experience the same with this box. It had to be exactly right, but he was finally satisfied.

He opened the lid to reveal the chains inside. They were soldered to thick metal bands around the bottom of the box. The perfect place for Levi to lay. But he was still struggling too much. The fight with Thomas had taken much of Lotan's energy, and he didn't want to risk this failing. He gathered up the chain tighter around his hands, twisting and pulling until Levi's eyes fluttered closed, and his thrashing stopped.

He wasn't dead. He didn't have the luxury. Lotan knew when to stop. He knew the line and how not to cross it.

Hoisting Levi into the box, he stripped away his jeans and tore open his shirt to reveal more of his skin; then he secured the chains around his chest, hips, thighs, and ankles. Holes on either side of the box and down at the end were just big enough to shove his hands and feet through. Working quickly, so Levi didn't wake up too soon, Lotan removed the chain from around his neck and set it aside. He went back to the front of the basement, following the sound of the chattering and squeaks. After three days in the trap with only water, they would be hungry. But Lotan would take care of that.

The flashlight showed the color in Levi's face was just starting to come back as Lotan got back to the box. He took a pouch from the bag secured across his chest and to his hip and opened it. The rats in the cage chattered louder, begging for the smell of the grains mixed with peanut butter as Lotan sprinkled the ground mixture over Levi. He then piled more outside the box on either side and down at the end. Rats are incredible little creatures. They seem so big until you see them condense and squeeze themselves through tiny spaces to get where they want to go.

Of course, even the most limber rat can find a space too small to pass through. Then he would have to gnaw his way through whatever is blocking him. That shouldn't be too difficult for them.

Lotan readied the lid of the box, and in one swift movement, opened the cage, placed it inside, and closed the lid. He draped the chain over the lid and set the shackles on either end to Levi's hands to secure them to each other. Connecting another chain to the center of the first, he brought it down and locked further cuffs around each of Levi's ankles. Finally, he pulled off his shoes, tucked his socks neatly into them, set them beside the box, and walked away.

He was nearly to the stairs when he heard the first screams.

Lotan let out a breath and walked away. A great pressure was gone from his chest. The bag he'd carefully packed that had at first pulled on his shoulder with its weight, now felt light. He didn't go back for the hook hanging near the pool. Instead, he made his way down the old access road behind the hotel and drove to the motel he'd chosen. He knew he wouldn't be seen coming back. By the time he got out of the hot shower, the morning was half over.

One more day.

He spent it cleaning the blood from the room and the inside of the stolen car he'd used. He ordered his favorite foods and watched TV. When night fell again, he took his bag and walked to a nearby convenience store. He drew his gun, pointed it at the man behind the cash register, then flicked his wrist and fired. The bullet buried itself in the advertising board behind the man now on his knees on the floor. It took only seconds to hear the sirens in the distance.

Five years.

In five years, he would walk free again, and there would be no trace.

No one would know, as they were tucking him away behind bars, that they couldn't hold him if he didn't want them to. A new name on his identification. A new backstory memorized in his mind. He could reclaim all he was when they set him free.

It was only five years.

## CHAPTER TWENTY-FOUR

NOW

The Sleepaway Hotel looks exactly like I remember it. Not that I really expected it to look any different. Places like this never change much, and that's part of what I like about them. It's nice to pull into the parking lot and get exactly what I was expecting, exactly what's in my mind. Right down to the skid of white paint out of the parking space where I hid behind my car a year ago.

"That's where I got shot at," I point out to Sam as we get out of the car.

He looks at me over the top of the car and raises an eyebrow.

"Where you got shot at?" he asks.

"Yes. The first time I came out here, actually."

"That's a lovely welcome," he mutters, shutting the door.

"Well, it was as I was leaving. And it wasn't the owner of the hotel," I explain.

"Who was it?" he asks.

"I still don't know," I say. "The official word from the Feathered Nest P.D. is a wayward shot from a hunter. Of course, that's the same thing they said about Ron Murdock when he toppled over onto my cabin porch dead. Apparently, there are just rogue hunters running wild out here?"

A gust of warmth and a friendly voice greet me when I step through the glass door into the hotel lobby.

"Hi, Mirna," I call in. "It's Emma."

"Agent Griffin, as I live and breathe," Mirna gasps, coming around the front counter toward me. She slows down as she gets closer, and the expression on her face drops slightly. "That's probably not a saying I should use when I'm talking about you."

I chuckle. "Don't worry about it."

"It's so good to see you, Emma," she says, finding her energy again and coming over to hug me. "I'm so sorry it's under these circumstances. I heard about that poor woman."

I listened to the same newscast and know for a fact it didn't give anywhere near close to the full story of what happened to Marren. It's for the best.

"It's good to see you, too." I gesture to Sam. "This is Sheriff Sam Johnson. Sam, this is Mirna."

"Nice to meet you, ma'am," Sam nods.

"Nice to meet you, too," Mirna says. She eyes him up and down. "Sheriff? You aren't here on any official business, are you?"

"Unofficial official business," I tell her. "There are two things I just want to ask you about."

"Go ahead," she says. "Can I get you a cup of coffee or anything?"

"No, thank you. I know it's been a while, and you're probably doing everything you can to block out what happened the last time I was here. But I need you to think back as carefully as you can. Do you remember when that man Ron Murdock came in here? The one who was shot at my cabin?"

She shudders. "Of course I remember."

"Alright. There's something I didn't think of before now. In all the upheaval of those few weeks, I missed a detail that could be extremely important, and I need you to try to remember for me. When he came in, did he tell you where he was from?"

"He filled out that card," Mirna says. "I remember it mysteriously went missing."

She looks at me with a slight smirk.

"I know he filled out the card. But did he tell you where he was from first? Before he filled it out?" I ask.

Mirna thinks for a few seconds, then shakes her head.

"No. I can't say that he did," she says.

"Are you sure? Think really hard about it. Remember when he came in and came up to the desk. Maybe you asked him his name and then where he was traveling from? Trying to strike up a conversation?" I lead, wanting to be completely positive in her memory.

She thinks again but shakes her head a few seconds later.

"No, I didn't. He was very quiet and standoffish. You remember the footage. He wanted as little to do with me as he possibly could have. It was all I could do to get him to fill out the guest registration card. I'm sorry if I'm not being helpful."

"Actually, that's very helpful. The next thing is more recent. It should be easier. And probably a little familiar," I continue.

"Are you going to ask me to look at my guest books again?" she asks.

"Yes," I tell her.

She stares at me, and I start wondering how long it would take to get the nearest court to issue a search warrant, but finally, she turns back to her desk and gestures for me to follow her.

"Just this once," she says.

"Hopefully, I'm never going to have reason to ask you again," I tell her. "Next time I come here, I would like it to be just as a guest."

"Any time," Mirna smiles.

Sam and I stand by the counter while she gets the book full of guest registration cards. She sets it down in front of us and waves her hands over it like Vanna White.

"Still using paper, I see," I observe.

"It's what I'm used to. Funny things happen with computers. Paper stays paper. Nothing beats it," she says.

"Scissors do," Sam comments.

We both turn to glare at him, and he shrugs. "Just an observation."

"Well, I've got a few things I need to do in the office. The scissors are planning an uprising, and I'm hoping to call in a few rocks to defend the paper. You call me if you need anything else."

Sam grins as she disappears into the office. "See? She gets it."

"Alright, here we go," I say, opening the book to the most recent check-ins and scanning through them. "It's not exactly a hopping tourist season around here. Not that there really is a hopping tourist season around here. Looks like we have some business travelers, though."

I let out a disbelieving scoff.

"What?" Sam asks.

I point to a name in the book.

"Andrea," I say, "is a waitress and bartender who works in the next town over. Checks in here a few times a month to screw LaRoche. I really thought she would have gotten that out of her system by now."

"Apparently not."

I continue to flip through the pages, not seeing anything familiar, until my hand stops. I can't believe what I'm seeing.

"Dean Steele," I say.

"The man from the train?" he asks, sounding as shocked as I am.

"The man sitting behind me who kept showing up where I didn't want him to be, then managed to slip out of existence before anyone could question him? He said he's a private investigator but wanted nothing to do with the investigation. Looks like we know where he went."

Mirna comes out of the office and looks between us.

"Did you find what you were looking for?" she asks.

"I think so," I nod. "Thank you for letting me look. I really appreciate it."

"Absolutely. And I meant it. Anytime you want a place to stay, or just want to come by and visit, you're welcome here."

"Thank you. I might be back by in the next couple of days," I tell her.

She smiles and nods as we head out of the lobby and back to the car. This time I get behind the wheel. Sam looks at me with expectation as I hook my seat belt and turn over the engine.

"What was that all about?" he asks. "Why did you ask her about Ron Murdock?"

"When it first happened, LaRoche was, let's just say, uncertain about me. He called me in to question me even though it was fairly obvious I had nothing to do with it. One of the first things he asked me was if I knew anybody in Florida."

"Why would he ask you that?" Sam asks.

"According to LaRoche, Murdock's driver's license has a Florida address," I tell him.

"But the address on the registration card was for Iowa," Sam points out. "You already told me that."

"It was," I confirm. "The Field of Dreams. That's how I ended up finding out everything about my father and the house there. When I left Feathered Nest, I had a vacation planned. I never really took any vacation time, so I built it up and decided I was just going to go. I went to Maine because of a tip about Greg, but the tip didn't pan out. So then I ended up in Iowa for a few days but had to be back in time for Jake's trail. I planned to go back to Iowa after giving my testimony."

"Is that the same trip you were trying to take again when I called you?" he asks.

"Yep," I say. "Notice I still haven't taken that trip. But the point is, why would LaRoche ask if I knew anybody in Florida when the address card said Iowa?"

"It is an interesting question," Sam muses.

"That it is," I agree.

We drive out of the parking lot and head down the road in silence for a few seconds before Sam turns to me again.

"Can I ask you a question?"

"No," I say. Out of the corner of my eye, I see him open and close his mouth, not sure where to go from there. I grin. "Go ahead. I just hate when people ask that."

"I'm sorry. Let me rephrase. I'm going to ask you a question," he says.

"Fire away," I tell him, glancing over my shoulder through the back window as I change lanes and take a turn.

"You told Nicolas the first sign of any engagement with the guy behind Catch Me was the video clip sent from Mary Preston's cloud," he says.

"And that would be a statement. Care to attach the question to the end, or should I just insert my own question mark at will?" I ask.

"As much as I'd enjoy seeing what you could do to an innocent sentence with a carte blanche question mark, I'll add it. Why didn't you tell him about everything that happened in Sherwood or in Quantico? About the necklaces, your mail, or the birth certificate being stolen?"

"Because it's not him," I say simply. "Catch Me is playing a game. It's all showy and dramatic. If he had the necklaces, he would have mentioned them again. He wouldn't just sneak into my house and not leave one of his notes. Besides, I saw the person's face."

"The man you thought was your father."

"The man I now know isn't."

"And you're sure he couldn't be doing both? Just to mess with you?" Sam asks.

"I'm sure. Catch Me has never mentioned Greg showing back up. He had the video clip of him, but that's it. He wouldn't have let someone else find him. Greg ending up like that on my front yard was a message to me. That means Catch Me didn't know it was going to happen, and the person who did it didn't know I wasn't going to be there. They aren't the same person. Which means I have to deal with both."

## CHAPTER TWENTY-FIVE

"Where are we going?" Sam asks a few minutes later, as we're still driving down the road and haven't gotten anywhere near going back to Feathered Nest.

"I thought we'd stop by a local bar for a drink," I offer.

"It's not even ten A.M. It's five-o'clock-nowhere," he says.

"Then I thought we'd stop by a local bar for a chat with a bartender," I tell him.

"Are you seriously that interested in the questionable morals of the chief of police?" he raises an eyebrow.

"At this point, I'm interested in just about everything," I answer.

We get to Lacy's, and I pull up in a spot I'm fairly certain is the same one I parked in when I was here the last time. Only then I was in a car that felt like I was holding it together by sheer will, and I walked out of the bar to discover my back seat covered with the broken glass of the destroyed outside light from the cabin.

Andrea looks up from the bar as we walk in. I can't say she looks exactly happy to see me. More confused and hesitant.

"Emma?" she asks.

"Hey, Andrea," I say. "How have you been?"

"What are you doing here?" she asks, then shakes her head, her eyes closing. "I'm sorry. That was really rude."

"It's fine," I tell her. "I'm back in Feathered Nest for a few days dealing with a situation."

"That woman's murder," she says. "It's horrible."

"Do you say that because you heard it on the news, or because Chief LaRoche is feeding you details?"

Her face drops, and she turns around to snatch a rag off the counter. The bar isn't even open yet; there's nothing for her to clean up, but she scrubs at the top of the bar aggressively anyway.

"Did you come all the way out here just to judge me?" she asks. "If so, I don't have anything to say to you."

I walk up to the bar and lean against it so I can get closer to her.

"I'm not judging you, Andrea. That's not why I'm here."

"Is he spreading rumors about me? Telling people I broke up with him?"

"You broke up with him?" I ask.

She pauses and looks at me.

"Yes. Last week. How did you find out we were seeing each other if he didn't tell you?" she asks.

"I saw your name on the guest registration cards at the Sleepaway Hotel. It seems you were meeting up with him quite a bit again," I tell her.

She goes back to angrily scrubbing at the bar, and I wonder which specific memories she's trying to obliterate from her mind.

"And that's what I told him. After everything happened with Jake Logan, I was so scared and confused and upset; I didn't know what to do. Adam said everything was going to be different. He apologized for the other girls and said he wanted to really try with me. But we were going to have to keep it quiet for a little while."

"Of course he did," I say.

Andrea makes a sound somewhere between a mirthless laugh and a sob. She throws the rag into the sink and leans her back against the bar, so she's facing me from the opposite angle, her arms crossed over her chest.

"And I believed him. I was stupid enough, and what I thought was in love enough to believe him. I really thought it was going to be different. It hurt so much to find out about him seeing those other girls, especially Cristela. But all I could think about was how buddy-buddy he had been with Jake. This person I thought I knew, who I thought was a dear friend, had butchered fifteen people. He stitched them together like throw pillows, then came to my bar and drank my bourbon with me. The more I thought about it, the more twisted it sounded, and I felt so guilty. I should have known something was wrong with Jake. He was here all the time, and I never picked up on it. And that got to me. It got to me a lot, and eventually, I just fell into what was familiar and comfortable."

"What happened? It's been a year," I point out.

"Exactly," she says. "It's been a year, and I'm still checking into a hotel three towns away from where he lives. At first, it made sense. With everything going on and all the heat on Feathered Nest and Adam, he didn't want to drag me into it. Didn't want the sensationalism of people knowing one of the victims was his ex-girlfriend, and he had another one. It was all too much. Staying under the radar felt safe. Like we could hide away from everything with each other. Then it just never changed, never got to normal."

"What would you need to hide away from?" I frowned. "You weren't involved in any of the murders."

"No, but my name was mentioned, and people figured out Jake came here. For months after he got arrested, some nights there were more reporters here than actual customers. That's actually what finally broke us up," she tells me.

"The reporters? I thought you said they were only coming for a few months."

"They were, then they stopped, and it felt like I could breathe. But then a week or two ago one of them came back. He'd come by a few weeks after everything like a lot of the others, but he was different."

"How?" I ask.

"Just the stuff he wanted to talk about," she says, absently pulling her blonde hair down from its ponytail and ruffling it before sweeping it up again. "Most of the other reporters wanted to talk about Jake and the crimes. Some of them wanted to play up how involved I was, and others wanted to focus on Adam. 'Corrupt Chief of Police Too Busy Bonking Bartender to Notice Serial Killer in His Town.' Those were fun ones. But this guy wanted to talk about you specifically."

"I'd think I'd be a part of it," I note. "I was a little bit involved in that case."

"Not you and the case. I mean, he asked about your involvement in the case, and if I knew anything about how you investigated if I knew you were undercover, did you tell me any trade secrets, those kinds of things. But then the questions started being more about you as a person and your life than about the case."

"Like what?" I frown.

Sam slides up beside me. The warmth of him is reassuring.

"About your parents. If I'd heard about them, and how I thought that affected you. About your boyfriend. Obviously, I didn't really have anything to tell him. I told Adam about it, and he was really angry. He said I needed to back off and just leave it alone. That he was tired of hearing about you. Then the guy came back last week and started asking questions again. He wasn't able to get the last article he wrote published, but he said he was working on something big for the one-year anniversary. He was getting a jump on it and wanted me involved. That so many people were trying to tell my story and put me in their version of what happened. I deserved to have my voice be heard. Adam was furious when he heard, and it turned into a huge argument. I eventually told him I couldn't stand him wanting to control me without wanting a real relationship with me, and we broke up," Andrea concludes with a sigh.

"What was the reporter's name?" I ask.

"Um," she thinks about it for a second. "Fisher."

"Is that his last name?"

"It's his only name. That's all he told me."

"What did he look like?" Sam asks.

Andrea shrugs.

"Tall. Dark hair. Kind of the classic description, I guess."

"Did he write anything down? A phone number or email address or anything?" I ask.

"No," she tells me.

I nod and reach in my pocket to give her my card.

"Thank you. I really appreciate your help. If you can think of anything else, call me."

We walk out of Lacy's and climb into the car. My head drops back against the headrest, and I roll it to the side to look at Sam.

"That's a little strange," he says.

"Who has a big feature for the one-year anniversary of a serial killer's arrest?" I ask.

He shakes his head, and we head back toward Feathered Nest.

## CHAPTER TWENTY-SIX

Nicolas is the only officer still at the cabin when we get back. He's sitting on the front porch, sipping from a steaming cup.

"Don't worry, it didn't come from the teapot," he says when he sees my expression as I walk toward him. "I made some coffee."

"Is there more?" I ask.

"Yes," he says.

Without another word, I walk past him into the cabin.

"Did you find anything?" I ask as he follows me into the kitchen.

I've already made my way through most of one mug of coffee and have my sights on a second. It feels like it's been an eternity since the cup from the bakery this morning.

"No. Like I said, it doesn't look like anything else was touched or disturbed. But I did think of something. When you mentioned spice, I knew I'd heard it. It was standing out to me for some reason, but I couldn't remember. Then it just snapped into my head. Before you stayed here, there was a man who was here for just a short while. He didn't even stay for the entire time he had the cabin rented."

"Clancy mentioned that to me," I tell him. "He was here about six months before I came and just left. He didn't say anything or even turn out the lights."

"Exactly. He brought most of his stuff with him, but there were a few things left, and so Clancy came to turn them in. He was convinced the guy would come back and say we'd stolen his property. I remember because I was the one who took the inventory and put it in storage," Nicolas tells me.

"I thought Clancy said he didn't leave anything. It looked like he just changed his mind and rolled out," I say.

"Clancy usually comes by if people forget things in the cabins. In this case, it really wasn't much. Probably slipped his mind. It's not like there were clothes and effects draped all over the cabin. There were only a couple of things left. A little bit of change, a loose button. But the one that I just thought of was a pendant. Like a dog tag, almost. It was under the sofa with its chain. It was broken like it got caught on something and snapped. The man must not have noticed when it fell off," he said.

"That's happened to me before," I nod. "I've had necklaces just snap and slide down my shirt without me having any idea what was wrong. What made you think of that?"

"It didn't have his name on it like I would expect to see it. I guess the only way to describe it is like it was a novelty necklace? Like something my sister had at her bachelorette party."

"What did it say?" I asked.

"Call Spice," Nicolas tells me.

"Was there anything on the other side?"

"I honestly can't remember. I want to say there was, but nothing big. Like a trademark or imprint," he says. "Anyway, I don't know why he had that, but that's what I thought of when you said that."

"Do you still have that tag?" I asked.

"It's probably still in storage at the station," he tells me. "The man never came back for anything, and as far as I know, we didn't get rid of it."

"Would I be able to see it?"

"I don't see why not. It's been there for almost two years. If he was going to come back for it, I reckon he already would have. I'll look for it at the station and bring it by when I have some time."

"Thank you," I say. "Oh, do you remember his name?"

Nicolas shakes his head. "No. I didn't have any occasion to meet him or anything. To be honest, the only time I actually knew he was here was when he was already gone, and Clancy brought by his stuff. But you should ask Clancy. He would be the one to remember if anybody does."

"I will," I say.

He starts toward the door, then stops and turns toward me again.

"You did get a hotel room, didn't you?" he asks.

"No," I say. "I didn't."

"You need to do that," he says.

"We are," Sam says. I start to protest, but he shakes his head. "Emma, no. I can see it on your face, and I'm telling you it's not happening. We're not staying here tonight. And you're not staying here while I'm gone."

"Gone?" Nicolas asks.

"I have to go back to Sherwood tomorrow," Sam explains. "I've taken all the time away as I can. But I'm not going to be able to go and focus on anything if I think you're here alone after this happened."

"I'll call Mirna," I relent.

There's no point in arguing with him. Besides, it's probably for the better. This guy's already proven he's willing to get up close and personal with me. I don't think he'll hurt me in a way that's so simple and underwhelming. He would do something much bigger, like blow me up on a train. But that's no reason to risk it.

Satisfied by my agreement to go to the hotel, Nicolas makes his way out of the cabin again. I'm reaching for my phone when it makes a sound to alert me to a new message. I don't recognize the number, and I'm surprised when I open the message.

*Hey, Emma. This is Andrea. I remembered something you might be interested in seeing.*

Bouncing bubbles on the screen tell me she's adding something, and an instant later, a video attachment shows up.

**Keely thought it was so glamorous I was being interviewed, she recorded it without him knowing. You can't see a lot, but you can hear it.**

Sam and I sit on the couch and hold the phone between us. I press the play button, and the screen fills with an image of Andrea behind the bar. It's obviously night, and the lighting isn't great, but she's easily recognizable in the glow of the neon lights above her head. There's the shape of a man in front of her, but his back is to the camera. Just as she described, he's tall, and it looks like he might have dark hair, but that doesn't really narrow down the population by much.

"Can you state your name, please?" the man asks.

"Andrea Layne," Andrea answers.

"It's good to meet you, Andrea," he says in a low, smooth voice. It's polished and rehearsed enough to be a professional reporter, but something still strikes me as odd about him showing up again. "Thank you for agreeing to speak with me today. As I said, I'm Fisher, and I'm working on a piece about the events in Feathered Nest."

"Can I get you a drink?" Andrea asks, always on duty.

"No, thank you," he says. "If we can just get started."

"Go ahead," she nods. "What do you want to know?"

"Just weeks ago, it was revealed the woman calling herself Emma Monroe and purporting to be considering moving into Feathered Nest was actually Emma Griffin, an undercover FBI agent assigned to work on the case. She was the one who eventually caught Jake Logan."

"Yes," Andrea says.

"And you and Jake were close," he says.

Andrea squirms slightly, busying her hands by pouring herself a glass of water from the soda fountain.

"We knew each other, yes. He came to visit me at work."

"Were you ever an item?"

"I thought this interview is supposed to be about Emma Griffin's case," she says. "What does my friendship with Jake Logan have to do with that? Practically everybody around here knew Jake."

"I'm just trying to get a view of what happened. I'm really interested in my piece standing apart from everybody else's. Everyone else is telling the same story, so a fresh perspective could be very powerful.

Speaking of perspective, how would you describe Agent Griffin's state of mind when she was here?" he asks.

"Her state of mind?" Andrea asks. "I'm not sure I know what you mean."

"Did she seem in control? Like she was thinking clearly and could make good choices? Was she impulsive?"

"I really didn't spend much time with her while she was here."

"Were you aware that Agent Griffin's boyfriend was taken less than a year before she was given that assignment?"

"No, I didn't know that," Andrea says. "That must have been really hard on her."

"Do you think it clouded her mind?" the man asks. "Now that you know what was going on, can you see any behaviors you might link to that?"

"I really don't know," Andrea says. "She really just seemed like a normal person to me."

The clip ends, and I feel like there's no breath in my lungs. I turn to Sam to see if he heard what I did.

"He said Greg was taken," I say.

## CHAPTER TWENTY-SEVEN

"Taken," I repeat. "He specifically says Greg was taken a few months before I was given the undercover assignment. How would he know that?"

"Could this have been the second interview?" Sam asks. "By now news has gone around about Greg reappearing in the way he did. It's obvious he didn't do that to himself. It would be easy to jump to the conclusion that somebody took him."

"No," I shake my head. "Think about what the reporter said. Just weeks ago. This is the first interview he did with Andrea. And at the time Greg had been missing for a year, but there was no indication anything was wrong or that there was any foul play. It was strange he was gone, and nobody expected it, but there had been no evidence at all of an abduction. Nothing to that effect has ever been mentioned on the news or discussed by the Bureau. In fact, that was something we all had to agree to."

"What do you mean agreed to?" Sam asks.

"When it became obvious, he hadn't just walked away for an afternoon, or that he wasn't taking a weekend to himself, but was actually missing, the Bureau had to take an official stand about it. Just like what happened with my father, there are questions because of his career. Maybe he's missing because he's actually on a work assignment, or maybe he's missing because he was involved in something and had to disappear. The Bureau had to come up with exactly how they were going to broach the topic of him being missing without giving away any sensitive information," I say.

"What type of sensitive information?"

"The cases he had been working on. Other cases the Bureau was handling. Creagan called a meeting, and we all had to listen to him lecture us on confidentiality and maintaining distance from the situation. It was like he was convinced the media was going to swarm the headquarters, and the integrity of the entire FBI would be compromised. It definitely seemed like he was far more concerned about the ongoing image of the team than finding Greg. Not that I think he didn't care that Greg was missing, but he always thought Greg was a little bit of an odd duck. I guess everybody did. He figured he would just end up wandering back one day, or somebody would stumble on him accidentally, and he would have a perfectly reasonable but somewhat mundane explanation for what happened."

"But then he didn't," Sam notes.

"No, he didn't. And we continued to find out together. It was the official stance of the Bureau he was missing, and it had nothing to do with his career. We weren't to discuss or get involved in any form of media unless it was directly approved. After a while, we just had to buckle down and keep believing it because there was nothing else to believe. I wasn't allowed to be a part of the investigation, so Eric kept me as informed about it as he could. He was completely confident Greg would show back up or we would find him."

"What did you think?" Sam asks.

"I didn't know what to think. But I found it really hard what to believe he would just venture off without telling anyone. But none of us ever said anything to the effect of he was abducted." I pull the phone closer, so I can try to get a better look at the still image of the man who called himself Fisher. Who is this guy?

Sam and I decide to go back to the hotel and try to get some rest. We are both worn out from the last few days, and I'm not looking forward to him leaving in the morning. I want to savor a little more time with him, knowing we will both be facing difficult things without each other. But no matter how much I try, I can't get my brain to quiet down. I lay there beside Sam, staring at the ceiling and willing myself to go to sleep. Everything keeps pumping through my brain, common questions, and their confusing answers. New questions. Ideas. I can't stop thinking about Fisher saying Greg was taken. It stands out and makes me incredibly suspicious.

Finally, my brain shuts down, and I fall asleep. By the time I wake up, several hours have passed, and I feel both better and worse. I hate that feeling. I lay down to rest because I'm exhausted and somehow end up waking with less energy and feeling more dragged down to earth. Climbing out of bed, I step in the shower and stand under the pelting water until it jostles my brain awake. Sam is up when I get out of the shower.

"What next?" he asks. "Where do you want to go?"

"We need to talk to Legends and Mayfield about the train bomb," I tell him. "We haven't even checked in with them since we left, and they need to know there's another element to the investigation now. The two jurisdictions are going to have to decide if they'll cooperate with each other or not."

"I would love to see Chief LaRoche and Detective Legends trying to cooperate with each other," Sam chuckles. "That's never going to happen."

"Probably not. But it would be really funny to see them try. Let's call him and see if there have been any further developments and fill them in on what's going on here," I say.

He agrees, and we pull up a video chat to speak to the detectives handling the murders and bomb threat from the train. Mayfield looks happy to see us like he always does, but there's a brooding look in Detective Legend's eyes that tells me absence hasn't made his heart grow any fonder when it comes to his perception of me.

"Emma, Sam," Mayfield starts. "It's good to see you two."

"Good to see you, too," I say. "How's the investigation? Anything new since we've been gone?"

"Are you askin' whether we've been capable of managin' our own investigation while you ran off on another whim?" Detective Legends asks. Always the charmer.

"I'm asking exactly what my words said," I tell him. "Have there been any new developments since Sam and I left yesterday? You apparently haven't been paying attention to the world around you, or you would know I didn't just run off on a whim. There was a murder in Feathered Nest, and it relates directly to what happened on the train."

"Notes?" Mayfield asks.

"Yes," I nod. "There was a note pinned to the clothing of the body, and one written in blood on her wall. Similar concept. Baiting me and telling me to catch him. It's obvious the two situations are linked, so I thought you should know what was happening."

"Thank you," the young detective says. "We'll get in touch with the local police department there and coordinate our efforts as much as possible."

"Sounds good. I think you could both benefit from information the other one can provide. I also wanted to let you know Dean Steele has resurfaced. I haven't interacted with him, but it seems he's been sniffing around outside Feathered Nest. If you're still interested in discussing the situation with him, I suggest you come here."

"We won't be doin' that," Detective Legends cuts in. "We have more than enough to keep ourselves busy here, and no time to waste."

"Detective Legends, I hardly think interviewing someone who witnessed at least one of the corpses and engaged with me at several points during the trip is a waste of time, considering what you're trying to do is piece together what happened on that train. Seems to me like he might be an important source of information."

"Miss Griffin—"

"Agent Griffin," I correct him, my voice cold.

"Agent Griffin, I thought I made it clear to you I don't need your help doin' my job," Detective Legends says. "You've been kept as a consultant out o' professional courtesy, 'cause you have direct insider knowledge about the situation. But you could just as easily be interviewed and sent on your way."

"Detective Legends, I do not purport to help you do your job," I say.

"That's a good thing because we wouldn't even compare."

"You're right about that. But I can't fault you. You just need some more experience, and I'm sure you'll improve."

Sam nudges me in the hip with his elbow, but I ignore him.

"Is there anything we can do to assist with your investigation there?" Mayfield cuts in, glossing over the tension between the other detective and me.

"No, thank you. But I'll let you know if anything comes up."

"Will do the same," he tells me.

We get off the call, and I pull up the video from Andrea again.

"What are you doing?" Sam asks.

"I'm going to send it to Eric and see if there's anything he can do about the lighting. I know Fisher's back is to us, but maybe he can improve the quality in some way so we can get more information from it."

Sam and I spend the next few hours going over everything again, trying to find connections when we decide to break for dinner. When my phone rings, I pick it up without looking at the screen, assuming it's the delivery driver down in the lobby with our dinner. Instead, it's Nicolas.

"I'm sorry it's taking me so long," he says. "But I still have the necklace. I can have it for you tomorrow if you like."

"That would be great. Thank you," I say.

"Oh, and I talked to Clancy. I happened to run into him and asked about the man who stayed there before you. He said the only reason he remembered the name is because it struck him so strange. Doc Murray. But he said he didn't seem like a doctor, so that must have just been his name."

"Tell him I said thank you if you run into him again before I do," I say.

"I will."

Shaking my head slightly, I turn to Sam. "The man who stayed in the cabin before I rented it went under the name Doc Murray. Think about it. Doc Murray. Murray Doc. Murr-Doc. What do you think of the chances there are six more Murrays at home with names like Sneezy and Dopey and Bashful?"

"Not good," he answers.

I nod solemnly.

"I didn't think so."

# CHAPTER TWENTY-EIGHT

## IAN

SEVENTEEN YEARS AGO ...

Even in spring, Vermont was so cold Ian felt like he never really escaped the chill. It was especially deep in his bones that morning when he woke up and opened his computer. The email at the top of his inbox was one he was expecting, but the impact of seeing it was more intense than he even anticipated. He stared at it for a long time before opening it. There was nothing in the subject line and nothing in the body of the email. There was only an attachment.

Eventually, he clicked on it. A scanned page of a newspaper filled the screen. Mariya's obituary. He read through it to see how it was worded, glad that he'd entrusted that to Grayson. At the bottom was the specific information he was anticipating when he first saw the email. The funeral and burial details. As he looked over them, he picked up the phone and dialed Grayson.

"Did you take care of everything?" he asked when the liaison answered.

"Exactly as you wanted," Grayson said. "I saw to the casket myself."

"And the weight?" Ian asked.

"Balanced. It shouldn't call any attention."

"Have you heard from him?"

"Yes. He called this morning. He said you haven't spoken to him since it happened," Grayson said.

"I haven't. And I don't intend to. He wasn't here. He was supposed to be and he wasn't. Mariya is dead because he didn't do his job," Ian said angrily.

"According to his manifest, he was where he was supposed to be. The plans changed at the last minute, and he responded as quickly as he could."

"Are you defending him?" Ian asked incredulously.

"You shouldn't hang onto anger that isn't justified," Grayson told him.

"My wife is dead. My child has no mother. I have to change everything about my life. Today I should be finishing filling Easter eggs and going to the grocery store for everything Mariya forgot for Easter dinner. I should be calling her to find out when she was going to get home, and making the bed with the new sheets I got her as a surprise so she could take a shower when she got home and slip into them to rest. Instead, I'm sitting in a cold, almost empty house with a devastated child who hasn't spoken a word in forty-eight hours, and I found out our host sent the Easter card from Mariya on Wednesday, so it will arrive in Virginia several days after her death. Any anger I'm feeling is justified."

"I'm sorry, Ian," Grayson said. "I need to go and get ready for the service. Do you want me to send you pictures?"

Ian felt bile rise up in his throat.

"No," he said. Before he hung up the phone, he hesitated. "Take them," he instructed. "Take pictures, but don't send them to me."

"Alright," Grayson said.

Ian hung up and walked to the living room. Emma was still curled up in the corner of the couch, wrapped in the blanket like a cocoon. She'd been there with very little movement since waking up in Vermont several hours after leaving Florida. The private plane arranged for them meant no one questioned the heavily sleeping child still in her pajamas or the tracks of tears on her face. The crew of the plane knew exactly what happened and what was being asked of them, even without him saying a word. The same was being asked of him now.

Emma didn't need to say anything, to make any noise or acknowledgment, to ask him to leave her alone. Another small dose of the sedative partway to Vermont kept her comfortable and secure during the trip. But it also left her confused and frustrated when she woke up. She would know she was somewhere different but remember nothing since lying down on the couch in Florida. After that, she moved from the bed to the couch and had been there with very little movement since still clinging tight to the blanket.

Ian knew the scent would go away soon. She would breathe the last of her mother's scent and then have to be without that smell for the rest of her life. So he would never ask her to take it off. She could lose herself to the cozy folds and the couch as long as he didn't lose her to anything else.

Without saying anything, he sat down on the far end of the couch and stared ahead. The TV was set at an angle, and when he looked at it, the corner of his eye still framed the mantlepiece of the fireplace. It was a beautiful spot, one made for setting up a Christmas tree and decorating altogether. In just a few more days, Mariya would be there. He'd place her there, so she was a part of everything they would do together. Then they would grieve.

## CHAPTER TWENTY-NINE

NOW

I don't want Sam to leave the next morning, but I know he has to. Sherwood can't be without its sheriff indefinitely; he has things he has to deal with there. Including dealing with the situation with Greg. The rest of the department managed to take care of the earliest part of the investigation and dealing with the public, but he needs to be there now to tamp down the rumors and try to create as much confidence in the town again as possible. It made it easier that he was transferred back to the hospital nearest to the Bureau as soon as he was identified. Without any family nearby, his emergency information lists Eric as his first point of contact if anything were to happen to him. It used to be me. That was one of those relationship milestones he put a tremendous amount of emphasis on. We were serious enough for him to list me as a person he wanted to be contacted if something serious were to happen to him.

He was never mine. I didn't tell him that, and now that I look back on it, I realize it was just another of those things that kept my distance from him. It makes my heart twinge a little every time I think of that. He should have had more. He seemed comfortable with our relationship exactly the way it was. That's why he was so safe. He didn't have passion and intensity that might have overwhelmed me. But what he should have had was a girlfriend who genuinely had more in common with him, and who would have wanted him first if there was an emergency.

Greg switched the contact information the day after he ended our relationship. I'm not sure why he chose Eric. They were friends, but not the type of close friends I could see giving that type of responsibility to each other. But I guess there wasn't really any other choice. He could have chosen his father, but he didn't even live in the state, and they weren't very close, and his only sibling was on a military tour. Eric was a good choice. They were friends and knew each other better than some of the other agents just because of their connection to me. Besides, Eric is a solid, steady, reliable person who he knew would be there as soon as he was needed.

And he was.

He went to Sherwood as soon as they called and had Greg transferred to the hospital near the Bureau as soon as they stabilized him enough to do it. Now he's near doctors who are already familiar with him and people he knows can be around him. It's the best thing for him.

But it created confusion and fear in Sherwood. All people knew was a man wrapped in bloodied plastic was found in my front yard in the days following the horror on the train, then he was whisked away without any information shared with them. Sam is their comfort, their trusted voice. He'll be able to calm them down and reassure them of their safety without giving away too many details.

I'll miss him. But fortunately, there is more than enough here to keep my mind busy. After the night in the hotel, we went back to the cabin so he could pack up the rest of his things. I stayed there after he left, waiting for another rental car to be delivered so I'd have transportation while I'm here. He doesn't like the idea of me being in the cabin, but I'm not going to stay cooped up in the hotel waiting all day. Once the car is here, I'll pack everything up and head out to talk to a few people.

It's not too long after Sam leaves when I finally hear tires crunching on the gravel outside. Assuming it's my rental car, I step out onto the porch. Instead, I see a squad car. Nicolas climbs out, and I walk down the steps to meet him.

"What are you doing here?" he asks.

"I didn't bring everything with me when I went to the hotel. Sam just left, so I'm getting a rental car delivered here," I tell him.

"You shouldn't be here alone," he says.

"It won't be for long, and I can protect myself. Besides, I technically have it reserved under my name for the next two weeks, and I know how much it bothers everybody when people leave before their time is up," I say.

"Speaking of which," he says, reaching into his pocket. "I have that necklace with me. Chief says he thought we got rid of that stuff a long time ago, so he doesn't want it back in storage. I guess you can hang on to it."

I take the broken chain and pendant from him and look down at it draped across my palm.

"Thank you," I tell him.

His radio crackles, requesting his attention at a call. He looks aggravated but confirms receipt of the message and that he's on his way.

"Don't stay here long," he says. "Technically, it's a crime scene."

"I know," I nod. "But nobody said I couldn't come back. I'll leave when the car comes."

"And you let me know if anything new happens," he says.

"Absolutely," I say.

Nicolas nods and gets back in his car, backing down the narrow road leading to the house for long enough that he's still pointing the wrong direction when I can't see him anymore. I'm walking back up the steps onto the porch when I hear the familiar snapping sound behind the house again.

Not hesitating for even a second, I take my gun into my hand and move around the side of the building, going in the opposite direction I hear the sound coming from so I can come up behind whoever it is.

As I turn the corner and continue around to the back of the cabin, I see a figure in the trees. I step out and aim my gun.

"Stop," I call out. "Keep your hands where I can see them and stay where you are."

The man does what I ask. Staying close to the cabin, I move along the back, passing him and coming around to his front. My jaw twitches when I see his face. Dark hair, blue eyes.

"Dean Steele."

"Emma," Dean starts softly, "lower your gun. I don't know how good your aim is, and I'd rather you not get spooked with it pointed right at me."

Without a word, I turn to the side, aim at a knot in a tree, and blow it away, then turn it back to Dean. He's a touch paler but still standing.

"Holy shit. What the hell was that?"

"A demonstration. What are you doing lurking around in the woods outside my cabin again?" I ask.

"I need to talk to you. The police were out here yesterday, and I heard over the scanner a car was coming out again, and I wanted to make sure you are alright."

"Why wouldn't I be?"

"Call it a track record," he offers, his hands still above his head. "Seriously, can you put the gun away?"

"Why are you in the woods?" I ask.

"It's the easiest way for me to get here. I found the path through from the railroad tracks."

"That's easier than driving?"

"It is when you don't want to be noticed," he answers.

"That inspires a tremendous amount of confidence in me," I tell him.

"I need to talk to you. Can you stand down for five minutes and let me talk to you?"

"Why didn't you stay at the train station to be interviewed like you were supposed to?" I ask.

"There wasn't time. Things needed to be done," he tells me.

"You were here the first night I got here, weren't you? Sam and I heard you going back through the woods."

"Yes."

"And you went into the cabin while we were back there," I say.

"Yes," he confirms. "Let me talk to you, and I'll explain everything."

"Why did you go into the cabin?"

"Because I needed to know for sure you are who you say you are."

## CHAPTER THIRTY

"What's that supposed to mean?" I ask, keeping my gun trained on him.

"Can we go inside and talk? I'd really rather not have this entire conversation standing out here with my hands in the air," Dean says. "Besides, it's really cold."

My spine stiffens slightly.

"Care for some tea?" I ask.

His head tilts to the side, and he looks at me strangely.

"No, thank you. I'm really more of a coffee guy."

The reaction seems genuine. Nothing in his face gives away that he knows about the teapot from yesterday. Finally, I lower my gun, and he gratefully drops his hands to his sides.

"Okay," I say. "You can have five minutes, but you better make them compelling."

I let him step in front of me so I can watch him as we walk into the cabin. He sits down on the couch, and I position myself at an angle away from him so I can see all his movements.

"Thanks," he says.

"Who are you?" I ask immediately.

"My name is Dean Steele."

"I know your name. Who are you?" I ask.

"I already told you. I'm a private investigator."

"And why exactly am I being investigated? Because I assure you there are a whole lot of people out there who know exactly who I am and don't need to creep around and commit burglary to confirm it," I snap.

"I'm sorry for going into the cabin, but I needed to make sure I was right. I've been looking for you for a long time," he says.

"That's not something you say to somebody who you want to trust you," I tell him.

"We have a connection, Emma," he says.

I stand up, ready to walk over to the door and firmly encouraged him to leave.

"I'm really sorry to disappoint you," I say. "But the position of obsessed stalker is already filled in my life. I really don't need to add another one to the roster. Though I'll admit you have gone to some pretty good effort, so if it wasn't disgusting, threatening, and a felony besides, I'd be touched. You can leave now."

"Emma, that's not what's going on. Not that kind of connection," he sighs.

Outside I hear a car pull into the driveway and gesture to the window.

"Look, my rental just got here. I need to pack up, and then I have things I have to do," I tell him.

"Because you'll be staying in the hotel from now on?" he asks.

I let out a breath. "Of course you know I'm staying there. I guess it serves me right for choosing the hotel you're also staying in."

"You chose the Sleepaway because you knew I was staying there?" he asks.

"Don't get too excited. We've been trying to find you since the train. It's pretty damn suspicious you just wandered off after lurking around me that whole time," I point out. "I'm going to call the detectives in charge of the case and let them know you're here so they can come interview you. Don't try to run again."

"Emma, we still need to talk," he says.

"I've run out of patience," I snap, starting for the door.

"When did your mother die?" he suddenly asks.

I turn slowly and face him.

"Excuse me?"

"When did your mother die? On the train, there were clues about your mother and the murder that just happened here, same thing."

"How did you know about that?"

"When did she die?" he asks, pushing past the question.

"I was eleven," I tell him.

"What time of day?"

"Is this fun for you in some way I'm missing?" I ask, readying my hand on my weapon again. This guy is getting on my last nerve.

"What time of day did your mother die, Emma?"

"The middle of the night."

"And you were home?" he asks. "Not out anywhere?"

"Of course, I was home. I was eleven years old," I tell him. "I was in bed when it happened."

"Then why do you remember walking through blood?"

The question hits me so hard I nearly take a step back.

"What?" I ask.

Dean reaches into his pocket and pulls out a folded piece of paper. Unfolding it, he holds it out to me.

"You did an interview a few years ago. You talked about your mother's death and all the unanswered questions about it, how there are differing accounts, and conflicting information that you've been trying to work through your whole life. You mention remembering getting back home and walking through her blood."

The knock on the door behind me startles me, and I whip around to face it. It takes a second for me to realize it must be the person delivering the rental car. Taking one more look at Dean, I go to the door and open it. The man outside smiles at me and holds out a contract on a clipboard. The name I scribble across the dotted line at the bottom might be more swirls than letters, but it works. He hands me the keys, gives me a wave, and heads back out to the car sitting behind my rental. I watch as he climbs into the passenger seat, and they drive away.

Closing the door, I walk past Dean and into the bedroom to finish packing. He follows me and stands at the doorway, waiting for a response.

"That was a nightmare," I explain. "It was a recurring nightmare. My therapist and I have talked through it, and she says it's normal to experience things like that after the trauma of a parent's murder."

"What if it wasn't just a nightmare? What if it was a memory that turned into a nightmare?" he presses.

"In that nightmare, I'm a teenager. It's the middle of the day, and I'm coming home from training at the gym. My mother died when I was eleven years old in the middle of the night. It can't be a memory, why are you asking me about this?

He ignores my irritation. "You said that there are conflicting stories about your mother's death. Different details and information you've gotten over the years that mean you aren't completely sure what happened, right?" he asks.

"Are you suggesting my mother was alive for years after I thought she was dead? That my father just concealed it?"

"No. but maybe it wasn't your mother. Maybe it was just someone who looked like her, but your mind turned it into her. I'm guessing you never saw your mother's body," he says.

I look up at him with all the rage I can muster, then look away.

"No," I sigh, tossing my clothes into my bag and rearranging them just so I don't have to look at him. "I saw the stretcher, but there was a sheet over her. I never even saw the room where she died."

"So, your mind wants to fill in that memory. What if what you think is a nightmare is a memory of finding someone else. Maybe someone who looks like this."

He takes out his phone, hits a few buttons, then turns the phone toward me. The image on the screen is a beautiful blonde woman with sparkling eyes and a wide smile. She looks so much like my mother; it makes my head spin, and I have to sit down on the edge of the bed. Dean comes toward me.

"Who is that?" I ask.

"This is my mother," he says. "She was found murdered, in an apartment registered to what turned out to be a fake name. An empty envelope was found underneath her, and there were two footprints made from her blood on the floor. They were made by a woman's athletic shoe. The complex wasn't outfitted with a security system, so there's no footage."

"When did this happen?" I ask.

"2008. I was sixteen."

Our eyes meet. His look so much like mine.

"In my nightmare, I walk into an apartment my father and I were staying in temporarily. There was a gym in the complex, and I'd just worked out. I expect him to be there when I go in, but he's not, so I go into the kitchen for a snack. My mother is lying there, blood everywhere. I look down, and my foot is in the puddle. The first time I had that nightmare, I woke up on the couch still in my gym clothes. My father was there, shaking me awake because he said I was screaming."

"No one ever identified the footprints in the apartment. There were only those two, none outside."

"I didn't have my shoes on when I woke up. When I found them in my room, they were clean." I let out a slow breath. "What happened to you after your mother died? Where was your father?"

"I never knew him."

## CHAPTER THIRTY-ONE

"You never knew him?" I ask.

"No," Dean shakes his head. "I never met him. It was always just my mother and me. But the way she talked about him, I knew there was something to the story she just didn't want to tell me. There are a lot of questions about my mother's past. I know you understand how that feels."

"I do," I tell him. "What kind of questions?"

"I don't know anything about her past. We have no family. No grandparents or aunts and uncles. No cousins. I haven't seen any pictures of her before maybe two years before I was born. Anytime I ever asked about her growing up, or our family, she found ways to talk around it. She said there wasn't much to tell, or she just didn't want to talk about it. It seemed like she was trying to hide something."

"And you could never let it go," I say.

"No," he says. "After she died, no one could tell me anything. The detectives did their best to be comforting and reassuring. They told me they would find out what happened and get the bastard who did that to my mother. All those things you hear on every police procedural TV show that's ever been made. The only difference is it actually means something when the characters say it. By the end of the forty-nine minutes, they've figured it out and tied everything up in a nice neat bow. The person who did it is either sitting behind bars or shot dead by a cop, and everybody goes on. But that's not how it worked out for me. They were never able to get any evidence that led them anywhere. There were footsteps in the blood and the envelope, and that was it."

"And there wasn't anything on the envelope?" I ask. "No DNA or handwriting?"

"Nothing," he tells me. "It was just an envelope. They don't even know if it came from the murderer, or if my mother had it for some reason. But they just kept telling me they would figure it out. They would find a break in the case and solve it. They wanted to put me in foster care, but I wasn't going to let that happen. I was sixteen and had been all but taking care of my mother for most of my life. Fortunately, friends of my mother's stepped up and said they would keep an eye out for me. The police accepted that, and for a while, they kept up with me almost every day. Then that turned to a couple of times a week, then a couple of times a month. Then, nothing. They couldn't figure anything out, so they just didn't want to talk to me. It's been that way since. And I decided I wasn't going to just let things like that happen anymore."

"That's why you became a private investigator," I say. He nods, and I mirror the gesture. "My parents are what inspired me to join the FBI."

"I know," he says. "I heard about you for the first time when your mother died. It was on the news, and it hit my mother really hard. I can still remember her sitting on the sofa, watching the TV, and just sobbing. When I asked her what was wrong, she just said the world is such a terrible place. That it was so unfair for a beautiful woman so young to have her life ended like that. And for her little girl to have to grow up without a mother. She was always sensitive, so it wasn't completely out of the realm of normalcy for her to cry over the news, but this was a lot. It was really tearing at her. I was only ten, and I was still able to recognize she was having a really strong reaction. A couple days later, I walked in on her on the phone. She didn't know I was there, and I distinctly heard her tell someone named Ian how sorry she was."

"Ian?" I ask. "My father?"

"I didn't necessarily put it all together at the time. It wasn't until I saw another news story and they mentioned his name. I asked my mother about it, and she said I must have misheard. But I know I didn't. Then years later, my mother was murdered. Like that horror she felt watching the news had manifested itself in her life. There were only a few tips about her murder. A few were just about where she was earlier that day, which didn't come up with anything useful. Then one said she was involved with drugs. And there was one anonymous tip that said to look into her past and gave a name," he tells me.

"What happened with that?"

"Nothing. The detectives told me they looked into it, but that the man named was dead and had been for some time. They wouldn't tell me his name, because I was still a minor and that man wasn't being accused of any crime, so they wouldn't release the information," he tells me. "It was all one big dead end. I tried to figure it out but nothing I did turned out anything. It wasn't long after that I heard the report that your father disappeared. I followed that story until it faded out of the news, too. Then I read that interview. I hadn't thought about your name in a long time. It only stood out to me because of your father's name. But as soon as I read it, it all hit me. I knew it was connected. I didn't know how or how to make anybody believe me, that I knew you had something to do with my mother's death," he says.

"Did you think I did it?" I ask incredulously.

"Did you think I killed those people on the train? Or the woman here in town?" he asks.

I stare back at him without answering, not knowing what to say.

"Exactly. The point is, neither of us know. I started digging into your past and mine, trying to figure out any overlap that might have happened before my mother's murder or after. There was nothing. Not until you came here."

"What do you mean?" I ask. "What did me coming here have to do with anything?"

"The first night you were here, a man died on your porch," he points out.

"I'm aware."

"He was never identified or claimed and ended up in a potter's field."

He's scrolling through his phone again, and I nod.

"Yes. Unfortunately. Ron Murdock. At least..."

Dean turns his phone around, and the breath escapes my lungs in a hard puff. The image on his screen is of a younger Ron Murdock standing beside a teenage Dean. His face is stern, but there's something almost affectionate about his posture. Dean's cap and gown are celebratory. His expression is sad and tired.

"At least that's the only name you could find for him. This is my high school graduation. That's Murdock, the friend of my mother's, who agreed to keep an eye on me after her death. We stayed in touch until I was eighteen."

"And then?"

"And then he left me a note saying he had to go, and I never saw him again," he tells me.

"Like a screwed-up Mary Poppins," I mutter, still locked into the picture.

"Only instead of him returning on an umbrella, he returned with a bullet in his back."

"And my name in his hand," I add.

"What do you mean?" he asks.

I look up at him, then cross the room to get my phone. Pulling it out of its case, I slip out the piece of paper I pressed there and bring it over to him.

"This was in his hand the night he died, right on the porch of this cabin," I tell Dean, showing him my name written across the ragged piece of paper. "I took it before the police came."

"He knew you," Dean says.

I nod. "I don't remember ever meeting him, but I have memories of him from when I was younger. Up until my mother died. I didn't think about him again until I found him on the porch and went to the hotel to find out his name."

"But we both know that's not his name. When it comes to that man, Ron Murdock doesn't exist," Dean says.

"I know."

His eyes drop to the broken chain and metal tag I didn't realize I am still holding.

"But whoever he was, he used to wear a tag that looked a lot like that," he tells me.

I look down at the tag on my palm, then flip it over, running my finger across the imprint near the bottom of the curve.

CM4. And just beneath it, a tiny green stone embedded in the metal.

## CHAPTER THIRTY-TWO

### ANSON

ONE YEAR AGO...

It took time and patience to get Travis to trust Anson enough to consider him a friend. From there, it was about connecting with Sarah. Travis shared her letters with him, and Anson raved over them, making the man feel important. More impactful than that, he made Sarah seem appealing. It didn't take a tremendous amount of intelligence or insight to see the way Travis looked at her. The adoration and attachment in her eyes weren't reflected back to her. Not that she noticed. All Sarah cared about was being close to Travis. He was everything to her, her complete devotion. Enough so that she didn't even think it was strange when he told her she couldn't come visit him at every visitation.

It would look suspicious, he convinced her. Even after his conviction, nobody linked her to him prior to his wife's murder. They didn't know he had a girlfriend. He protected her. He kept her safe so no one would suspect her of having anything to do with the crime they accused him of. Because, of course, he didn't do it. It wasn't him. All the evidence they had was faked. They planted it and came up with it because there was no other way for them to close the case. It was taking so long it made the police department look bad. They'd already had to call in the FBI, and they couldn't bear the thought of not being able to solve the case. Especially not the new agent they assigned to it.

It was all Emma Griffin, Travis told her. She had it out for him from the moment she met him. It didn't matter to her if it was true or not; this new agent was going to make sure he was convicted of murdering Mia and put him away for life. It wasn't supposed to be that way for the two of them. If only Mia hadn't disappeared and been murdered, he was going to divorce her and be with Sarah forever. So when his wife left him and so much suspicion fell on him, Travis had to do the only thing a good man would do and defend her.

But it didn't work, and he still ended up behind bars. But that didn't mean Sarah had to get wrapped up in it. As long as they kept their distance just enough, at least for now, no one would notice their relationship. They could pretend they just met and were gradually getting to know each other better, then come forward with their love.

Sarah believed him. Anson didn't.

There was somebody else. Travis hadn't told him who yet, but he would. There was another woman in the picture who knew what he'd done. Because she was there to help him. The letters she wrote to him, Travis never let anyone else see. The woman who put money in his books and sent him every perk and comfort allowed to him. The woman who came on days when he told Sarah not to visit.

So, gradually Anson moved in. He took his time and built up a rapport with her. They talked while they waited for visitation, then sometimes during it. Eventually, they ended up meeting up outside the prison to keep talking after the visitation was over. That's when he started to tell her more about Emma Griffin. The kernel of suspicion and hatred was already there inside Sarah. All it took was a bit of a nudge from Anson and it grew.

Travis couldn't have committed that murder, he told her. That's not the type of man he is. She knew him. She knew how gentle and loving he was. How kind and compassionate. He wouldn't do something like that to the woman he had married. No matter what type of person she was. No matter how miserable she made him or how badly she treated him. No matter how many times she cheated on him and withheld any sort of affection from him. Travis would never be capable of something so horrible. The only explanation is that he was framed.

But Sarah could fix it. She could get Travis out and grant him a new trial. He would be able to defend himself and prove those who falsified evidence against him had been constructs of a twisted and unreliable mind. All she had to do was prove it. And Anson would help her. He could get her all the information and everything she needed to make this all better. It would only be a little while longer. She just needed to be patient a little while longer.

Every time, she would ask: "How can I repay you?"

Every time, he would simply offer a smile and soothing words.

"No worries, Sarah. It's what friends are for."

## CHAPTER THIRTY-THREE

NOW

The next hour is a feverish flurry of phone calls and emails. I fill Dean in on the paper roses, and he immediately goes to work trying to track down the medical center to request records while I get in touch first with Clancy, then with Eric. Using the few details the aging handyman can remember about the man called Doc, I ask Eric to run a search for cold cases starting in May two years ago. I want him to look for any reports or cases involving a slim blond man in his mid-to-late forties who may be using the name Murray or Doc. I'm not surprised he immediately catches on.

"Another anonymous man using a version of the same fake name got near that cabin and left mysteriously?" he asks. "Feathered Nest needs to burn that place to the ground."

"That won't help this man," I say.

"At this point, we're only assuming that isn't his real name. Yes, it would be a coincidence on a massive scale for somebody named Doc Murray to stay in the same cabin where a man named Murdock dies six months later, but it's possible. If you don't know that, how are you sure he's actually missing?" Eric asks. "Maybe he just wasn't pleased with the amenities and wanted to write a scathing Yelp review."

"Find me the review and I'll believe it. Until then, I'll be more concerned that this man checked in and then was suddenly gone. No notice, didn't say anything. Didn't even turn the lights off or lock the door. And he left behind a broken necklace that links him to Murdock, to me, and to everything else. I don't know how or why, but that's what we have to figure out. And that starts with finding out what happened to him," I say.

"Is there anything else about him? Did he show an ID? Use a credit card? Give an email address? Maybe he visited a store in town and bought something," Eric says.

"This is Feathered Nest, Eric. They don't check ID for someone renting a cabin. It would never occur to them someone would lie about who they are, and it would seem offensive to try to verify it. He paid for everything with cash. No contact information."

"I'll do my best," he sighs.

"Thank you." I start to end the call, then push the phone back to my ear. "Eric?"

"Yeah."

"Check in Florida, too."

I get off the phone just as Dean comes back into the room. He's holding a piece of paper, and I see notes jotted on it.

"So, I searched around, and it turns out the hospital in Rolling View closed a few years ago," he explains. "And the doctor listed on her records retired at the same time."

"Perfect," I sigh. "So, there's nobody to request records from is what you're telling me."

"Well, there's no official person to request records from," he clarifies.

"What's that supposed to mean?"

"The hospital closed. But it was never demolished. It's still standing. Which means its record room could be intact," he tells me.

"Aren't medical records all on computers now?" I ask.

"Now," he says. "But these records are from thirty years ago. For a woman who died twelve years after that."

"So, her records probably wouldn't have been merged onto a computer," I say.

"Exactly. Just like the paper you found in the book, your mother's medical records are most likely pages in a manila envelope. And as unfortunate as it may seem for some people, decommissioned hospitals tend to not put a lot of emphasis on transferring hundreds of pounds of paper patient files. Especially ones for patients who aren't going to need them anymore," he says.

"They wouldn't shred them?" I asked.

"They might have," he says. "And they might not have. I've seen my fair share of abandoned hospitals, treatment centers, nursing homes. More of them than you would think look like people just walked out of them and forgot they were there. They still have beds with the linens on them, hospital gowns, and blankets stacked up in the cabinets. There's a point when the time and financial investment it would take to actually move the things isn't worth it. They would rather just close up shop and head to their sparkly new facility, leaving the past behind. And that includes patient files."

"But how would we know that? If the hospital has been abandoned for years, who's going to know if the record room is still intact? And who would we request the files from?" I ask.

"Let's just say after my stint in the military, there's a reason I became a private investigator and didn't go into law enforcement," he says.

"You were in the military?" I ask.

He nods. "Army. Delta Force."

"Wow. That's impressive," I raise an eyebrow. Admittedly, it didn't fit my early impression of the man.

"I didn't really have anywhere to go or anything to do after I graduated high school. A recruiter had come to the school to talk up the Army, and after graduation, I decided to go talk to him. It was somewhere to go, something to do. The military would pay for my education. And for a person with no roots and a bleak past, the structure and unity were nice. I ended up loving it, and it just went from there," he says.

"But you're still so young," I point out. "Why did you decide to leave?"

He lets out a softly pained, mirthless laugh.

"I didn't decide. The Army decided for me." I look at him questioningly. "I was involved in a secretive operation that didn't go exactly as we planned. I came out of alive, but just barely. The injuries combined with the length of my career already made them decide it was time for me to get my patriotic thank you and head on down the road."

"Oh," I say. "I'm sorry that happened to you."

Dean shrugs that off. "No reason to be sorry. I found my way." A nostalgic smile bends his lips just slightly before he continues on in a louder, stronger voice. "What's next?"

"I think I'm going to pack everything up and bring it to the hotel. Then we keep heading through the looking glass and find Alice," I tell him.

Dean helps me pack the rest of what I have in the cabin and put it in the car. He climbs in with me, and I drive him in a loop out of Feathered Nest and to the spot at the train tracks where a gap in the trees leads to the path through the woods. Being there again brings me right back to standing there more than a year ago, comparing the crime scene photographs of Cristela Jordan's body with the area around me. The blood and other remnants of her had long since been washed away, but there were still evidence markers and broken tree limbs to show the lingering aftermath. That's how I pieced together what happened to her. That she ran from the trees and was hit by the train rather than having been thrown in front of it as was the original theory.

It meant she was a survivor. Even though her life ended that night, she managed to escape from Jake's clutches and not become a piece of the grotesque museum to human suffering and misery in his basement.

Dean's car is sitting almost in the same spot I'd parked mine when I came here. He gets in, and we wind our way through the back roads to the hotel. Mirna pops out from behind the desk when we walk into the lobby.

"You found her," she says, looking at Dean.

"You asked about me?" I ask.

"I noticed your car here yesterday and thought you'd come by. But Mirna here was nice enough to let me know you checked in," he says.

"Did Sheriff Johnson already leave?" Mirna asks.

I nod. "This morning. He texted me a little bit ago to let me know he'd gotten home safely."

"That's a good man."

"I think so. Well, I'm going to go ahead and get this stuff up to my room. More work to be done," I say.

"Before you go, I have something for you," she says, heading back for the desk.

"Oh?"

"You got some mail."

"I got mail?" I frown.

She nods, sifting through a stack on her desk and pulling something out. She eyes it, then looks at me.

"Yep. It's postmarked yesterday. Must have gotten it in right in time," she says.

I take the postcard from her hand and look down at it.

"Thank you," I manage and head for the elevator.

Dean follows me into my room.

"What is it?" he asks.

I show him the postcard.

"The whale exhibit in the Smithsonian," I tell him.

"Is there anything written on it?" he asks.

I flip the card over. "It's good to be home. Come for a visit? Catch me if you can, Emma." A shiver rolls down my neck. "Son of a bitch."

Dean looks at the card and points to a printed label affixed to the bottom of the card.

"That's an access link," he says.

"To what?" I ask.

He takes out his phone and opens a browser.

"Let's find out."

He types the code in, and a few seconds later, a video stream appears. It's from an angle as if the camera is positioned in the upper corner of a room.

"Oh, god," I gasp.

"That's a hospital room," Dean says.

"That's Greg," I tell him. "And he's alone."

## CHAPTER THIRTY-FOUR

### GREG

FIVE MONTHS AGO...

"Are you absolutely sure you can't come with me?" Finn asked. "If there's anybody who should be getting out to do these things, it should be you."

"I know, but I can't," Greg said. "Not now. He's been watching me like a hawk. There's no way I would have enough time alone without him noticing. He's angry after what happened to Emma. It offended him that a cult would think they would deserve her."

The words came out of his mouth bitter and slimy. They were so much a contradiction; there was so much irony to hear Lotan rage about the immorality and horror of the Society for the Betterment of the Future, the cult Emma found herself tangled up in during her most recent investigation. The more they found out about what she faced, the angrier and more indignant he became. It was impossible to understand how he didn't see the parallels of what was happening.

The cult was led by a man who believed himself above every mere human who walked the planet. Indeed, he thought of himself as a God. He truly believed he was the embodiment of the divine represented on Earth, a direct connection between the chosen members of his organization and the intangible spiritual realm so many hungrily sought after.

But there was a very distinctive difference between the two groups. What Lotan and Leviathan destroyed on a large scale mostly impacted random people, the Society did it to precise individuals. Their evil was focused intently and unwaveringly on the specific people chosen for their leader's spiraling realms of hell.

Leviathan aimed at creating mass chaos and destruction that forced those people who happened to be caught up in it to find a way to cope if they survived at all. The Society aimed at isolating themselves away from the outside world and focusing only within, so those special few could enjoy the spoils. The destruction and pain was done within their walls.

But there were similarities. Each of the people chosen for its ranks were selected and groomed. They were carefully identified from among the masses and drawn in with careful promises. Either to destroy or to be destroyed. It's what the Society tried to do to Emma. It's what Leviathan did to Greg.

But he understood what was happening now. He wasn't going to let it continue. Lotan might have thought he had Greg firmly in his grasp, but he hadn't broken him. Greg could have chosen a different path. When Lotan had first brought him into the organization, he'd showed Greg so much favor. He was one of the honored few, high in the ranks even from the very beginning. He didn't have to earn his way or prove his devotion. Who he was and his association with Emma was enough to grant him a place by Lotan's side. He could have accepted that. He could have been enticed by the power and spoils offered to him. The world was being held out in front of him. Lotan had made it very clear he could do and have and be whatever he wanted.

All a reward for being one of the movement. A turning gear in the machine of chaos. It would have been so easy. There wasn't a fiber of Greg's being that didn't believe there were plenty of people who wouldn't have hesitated for a second. As soon as they saw the power Lotan wielded and heard what he was capable of offering them, they would have been seduced. Even people he considered friends, good men he trusted, and who had done amazing things for many people, would have crumbled.

If there was one thing Greg would learn from what he was facing now, it was to be more cautious with who he trusted. It seemed like such a simplistic concept, but it meant something deeper. He would no longer be able to see the world in the same way, both for good and for ill.

He continued to fight. Even when it would be easier not to. Even when it would be easier to think only about himself, he had to keep his mind strong. He couldn't let Lotan win. But that was much more difficult now. He was no longer honored, no longer considered among the most valued and important. Instead, he was a tool, a device being used in gradual slow doses to get Lotan to what he truly wanted. Emma. He had a plan for her, one that would destroy her and everything in her life. A plan crafted under the guise of love.

But the love of a twisted mind and tainted soul was as unstable as it was misled. The stronger it got, the more intense it got, and the closer it got to detonation.

Greg couldn't stop it. Not from where he was, under the constant watch of the piercing, increasingly wild eyes that checked in on him regularly. But he could slow it down. He could maintain enough control to let Emma unravel the tangled web of her past, so she could preserve her future.

So, he couldn't escape. He couldn't take Finn up on his offer. He was desperate to leave Lotan's clutches. Every bit of him cried out to not be here anymore. His body was damaged, his mind warped. He ached to be back in the world he knew and the life he had before any of this happened. But that was gone now. That possibility disappeared the night he walked away from that life. Lotan had beaten him down time and time again. All he could do was rise up.

But he had to do it from here. He had to force himself to watch Finn leave, to take the last remaining hope of escape. Because if he escaped, there would be no filter for Lotan's blind devotion and no way for Emma to get out of his grasp. Greg had to stay where he was and pull the threads for her one at a time. He'd tried at the bus station, but a bombing that wasn't supposed to happen meant his message would never get to her. He'd had to watch the television reports about her and know he hadn't reached her.

Watching those reports was one of the hardest things he had to do, and yet he wouldn't skip them. Even on the rare occasions he wasn't forced by Lotan to sit with him and answer questions he believed Greg could answer, he would still watch them. They were his connection to her, his way to know she was still alright, to see a glimpse of the world without the haze of blood. But it also forced him to see the pain she was enduring. He could only hope he could help take little bits away. And maybe he would survive to see it.

Tonight, he had that chance.

"You remember what I told you?" Greg asked.

Finn nodded.

"Yes."

"When you're at the funeral home, try to get as much information as you can about Mariya Presnyakov's funeral. Don't be surprised if they don't give you much. The most important thing is to write the name I told you in the guestbook. Make sure they will remember you were there," he said.

"How can you be sure she'll find it?" Finn asked.

"I can't be. All I can do is make sure it's there to be found."

## CHAPTER THIRTY-FIVE

I have no idea what's in my suitcase. I threw everything in there together so fast I didn't pay attention. It's entirely possible I have nothing but underwear and t-shirts, but that doesn't matter right now. I'm already on the road, leaving the cabin and Feathered Nest in my rearview mirror. Dean is still there. He will look into my mother's medical records and be there as my stead if something else comes up in the investigation. Nicolas isn't happy about it. He tried to keep me in town, but there's nothing that can stop me. I'm not a suspect. I'm not being held or detained in any way. I'm the one who asked to be part of the investigation. The crimes revolve around me, but that doesn't mean I have to be locked in place. Until there's a legal reason for it, they can't stop me.

And even if they did have a legal reason, I can't be sure I'd pay attention to it. Not now. Not when the live stream of Greg's hospital room is still ticking away on the screen of my phone, and no one is there with him. In the half an hour since I first watched the video, I've called both Bellamy and Eric at least five times each. Neither of them have answered, and I haven't gotten any response from my messages.

I've tried to call the hospital, but they won't talk to me, either. I'm not family, and I'm not on the authorized list given to them by the

Bureau. They are for all intents and purposes, his legal representatives at this point. He has no one else to advocate for him; no one else to ensure he gets through this in the best way possible.

And no one to be there for him.

Finally, my phone rings and I smash the button to answer it.

"Why aren't you there?" I ask.

"Emma? What's wrong?" Eric asks. "I'm sorry I missed all your calls. I had to go to a conference."

"Where is Bellamy?" I ask.

"She's here with me," he says. "What's going on?"

"Nobody's there," I tell him. "Nobody's at the hospital with Greg."

"How do you know that?" Eric asked. "Did they call you?"

"No. I got a postcard from my creepy pen pal. He's apparently taking a road trip and stopped by the hospital to plant a security camera. He sent me the link. It's a live stream of Greg's hospital room, and there isn't anybody there with him."

"That's not right," Eric says. "Jones and Calmati are supposed to be there today."

"You need to find out where they are and what's going on. This guy is there. I'm on my way. I'll be there in a few hours."

My next call is to Sam.

"I got a postcard from Catch Me," I tell him before he can even get a word in. "It had a link in it showing me a live stream of Greg's hospital room. Nobody's there with him. Apparently, Eric and Bellamy had a conference they had to go to, and they left two agents in charge, but they aren't there. I'm on my way to the hospital. I just wanted to let you know what was going on."

"Do you want me to come?" he asks.

"No. I can't ask you to do that. You need to be there taking care of Sherwood. I will let you know if anything else happens," I tell him.

"Have you been able to find out anything else in Feathered Nest?" he asks.

I already spoke to him earlier to fill him in on Dean and what was happening. There was a defensiveness in his voice when I told him that struck me as odd. I didn't get into it with him, but I sense some of it creeping back into his voice now.

"Dean is going to find out what he can about the hospital and try to access my mother's medical records. He's also going to do as much digging around town as he can. He's a private investigator, so he should be able to get some ground covered."

"And you're sure you trust him?" Sam asks.

"No," I tell him honestly. "Of course I don't. But right now, I don't have the luxury of only having people around me who I trust. He's the closest thing I can get who's also willing and able to help me. I still don't know who he is, Sam. I don't know why our lives are connected the way they are. But what I do know is I'm more likely to find out the things I need with his help than I am without it. And I'm going to have to take that chance now. I put off going to the hospital to see Greg and now this is happening. I've got to get there," I tell him.

"Tell me when you're safe," he says.

"I will."

I drive at breakneck speed the rest of the way. It feels like the hours keep getting swallowed, and I'm not making any progress, but after long, agonizing hours of empty roads, I finally start recognizing the landmarks. I'm getting closer. I'm twenty minutes away from the hospital when I glance over at my phone again. Everything has been calm and steady up until now. Nothing's changed except for an orderly coming into the room to check Greg's vitals. But now I see movement on the screen. There's someone else there. I briefly have a moment of relief. Maybe one of the agents who was supposed to be there all day has finally arrived.

But that feeling is short-lived. The figure walks up to the edge of the bed and leans over Greg, bringing his face to within inches of his. It takes only seconds for me to recognize him, just as he reaches out to touch Greg's IV.

I snatch the phone off its holder to call Bellamy

"You need to get somebody there now!" I scream. "He's there. The man from the picture is in the room with Greg. Get somebody to that hospital right now. Stop him!"

I end the call and throw my phone into the passenger seat. If I don't, I'll continue to watch the screen. I need to be paying attention to the car and the traffic in front of me. My heart pounds so hard in my chest; I feel sick. My sweaty palms make it difficult to keep my grip on the wheel. I struggle through the last of the traffic and finally pull into the parking deck at the hospital. Throwing myself out of the car, I run inside.

The twenty-minute ride has taken me almost half an hour because of traffic. It felt like an eternity. Anything could have happened in that time, and questions race through my mind as I run up the stairs to Greg's floor. A nurse stops me before I can get through the door.

"I need to get in there," I tell her, gesturing toward the floor behind her.

"I'm sorry. This floor is currently on lockdown. Access requires authorization."

"My name is Emma Griffin. I'm with the FBI."

She seems to contemplate this for a second, gauging if I'm telling her the truth. I pull my badge out of my pocket and show her.

"Is Agent Martinez here?" I ask. "Get him."

She disappears from the door for a moment, then returns with Eric. He immediately reaches for my hand as if to pull me through the door.

"Let her in. She's authorized," he instructs.

"Yes, sir," she agrees.

She steps out of the way, and I barrel out of the stairwell. The first thing I see is Bellamy. I run for her, and she grabs me in a tight hug.

"Did they get him?" I ask.

She shakes her head as she steps back from our hug.

"I'm sorry, Emma. I'm so sorry. By the time any of us could get here, there was no one in or out of the hospital that matched the description," she says.

"He was here," I insist. "I watched him walk through Greg's room. Is he alright? Has anyone checked on him?"

"He's fine. As soon as we heard from you, we called and had them put the floor on lockdown. The nurses went in and checked him completely, but there doesn't seem to be any changes."

I pull out my phone and turn the screen toward her.

"Shit," Eric murmurs.

I use my finger to back up the stream to the point the man came into the room. They watch for a few seconds before I can't take the anger anymore and whip around to face the desk.

"I want to know how the hell something like this happens," I demand. "There is supposed to be someone with him at all times. No visitors. How do you let something like this happen?"

"Emma, I called Jones and Calmati. They said the hospital called and released them from their posts for today," Eric tells me.

"Did they say who it supposedly was?" I ask.

"No."

I'm seething. I take a few deep breaths, struggling to bring myself under control.

"Where is his room?"

She leads me down the hall and to a closed door. A piece of paper slipped into a flimsy frame on the front of the door has Greg's name written. Like he's just moving into his college dorm and the RA wanted to welcome him. I have the compulsion to yank down the piece of paper involved and crumple it into a ball, but I stop myself. Instead, I open the door and step inside.

## CHAPTER THIRTY-SIX

My breath catches as I walk into the room and see Greg for the first time. I've been watching him on the stream, but that wasn't enough to give me a full picture of his real condition. I don't know what I was expecting, but what I see lying in that bed is brutal. Eric steps up beside me and places his hand on my lower back.

"You don't have to," he says. "I know it's really hard to see him like this."

I straighten my spine and shake my head.

"I'm fine," I tell him.

I step away from his touch and walk to the side of the bed. Greg's almost unrecognizable. If I didn't have absolute confirmation of it, I would probably struggle to see the features I know. It's been two years since I saw him, but it's not the years that have taken the face I was so familiar with. He's swollen and discolored. The bones of his face are broken in several places. Bandages wrapped around his head conceal most of his hair and stretch down over one eye. Tubes and wires create a web around him, connecting him to the machines functioning for him.

He's just sleeping. It's the first thought that flutters through my head, but I instantly push it away. In the logical part of my brain, I know that's not true. They've pumped him full of medication to keep him unconscious so his body can piece itself back together. Being awake would be too much of a strain. Would threaten to tip the delicate balance of his survival to the wrong side. So they have to sedate him, keeping him in a constant state of deep sleep just so he can stay alive.

One arm rests on top of the blanket draped over him, and I see stars sticking out from beneath the cuff of his long sleeve. Bellamy steps up beside me and stands silently until I'm ready to talk.

"How does he compare to when he was first found?" I ask.

"Some ways better. Some ways worse," she says.

I understand completely. The most traumatic injuries look the least severe when they first happen. Their intensity is only revealed over time. I can imagine much of the damage done to him occurred very soon before he was dumped in my front yard. That means the full effect of those injuries weren't yet apparent and are only now surfacing.

Paying attention to the angle of the bed, I turn around and let my eyes sweep over the seams connecting the walls to the ceiling. The view of the stream narrows down where the camera could be positioned, but I can't see it.

"Where's the camera?" I ask. "Where is it?"

"I don't see one," Bellamy says.

"Let me look," Eric offers.

Technology is his area of expertise, so I trust him to know better than I do what to look for. While he starts examining the room, I turn back to look at Greg. Emotions course through me, but I'm not sure what they are or what to do with them.

"You know," I comment to Bellamy. "I've thought about what it would be like to see him again so many times."

"I know you have," she says, her voice soft and comforting.

"I've tried to imagine different scenarios. What it would be like if he had just voluntarily walked away because he decided he wanted a different life. What it would be like if he did something horrible and was taken away because of it. What it would be like if something horrible happened to him. I tried to figure out how I would feel and what I would think when I was looking at him again."

"Is it like you thought?" she asks.

"No," I admit.

She draws in a breath and lets it out in a tremulous ribbon as she stares down at Greg. They were never close. It wasn't that they didn't get along or disliked each other. They just never particularly meshed or found any common ground. Bellamy thought he was insufferably boring, and Greg thought she was flaky and disconnected. Neither one of them were completely accurate in their evaluations of the other, but it kept them from forming any type of real friendship.

But now I can see a strange change has come over Bellamy. She's looking at him. Not just with a sense of duty and responsibility like I would expect, but with compassion and sadness. His attack has clearly been hard on her. She's trying to process not just the brutality of it, but the currently unknown explanation behind it. This wasn't just a random assault, or even a targeted onslaught that happened and was over. Greg has been gone for two years. We don't know how or why he was taken, and we're only just beginning to know what he went through.

"What are his injuries?" I ask.

"Emma," she says cautiously like she's warning me against myself.

"Bellamy. I don't need you to protect me. Not from this. What are his injuries?"

"I'll ask a doctor to bring in his chart," she says.

She walks out of the room, and Eric comes over to me.

"I think I might see where the camera is, but I need a ladder. Are you going to be alright in here by yourself for a minute?" he asks.

"Stop," I sigh in frustration.

"Stop what?" he asks.

"You know what I'm talking about. Stop looking at me like that. Stop talking to me like that. You can't shield me. That doesn't help. I'm here because I need to be. Because the waste of breath and flesh who did this didn't start with Greg, and he's not going to stop with him.

You know that as well as I do. You also know the only reason this happened to Greg is because of his association with me. Trying to insulate me from the reality of this will only make it harder for me to stop it from happening again. Now go get your damn ladder," I say.

Eric gives a single nod as he backs away.

"Understood," he says.

When he's gone, I walk around to the other side of the bed and sit in one of the two chairs pulled up near Greg's head.

"Mind if I sit?" I ask. As if he could hear me.

After a second, I sit, staying at the very edge of the cushion. "You know, that's one of the first things you corrected me on? You corrected me on a lot of things. Let's be honest; you correct everybody on a lot of things. But the one I remember from when we'd barely met was when you came into my office and just stood there. I was in the middle of doing something; I don't remember exactly what. But I only looked up when you came into the office, then looked down again, so I didn't realize you were just standing there for probably a full minute. I glanced up at the chair, and you weren't sitting. So, I looked at you, and you were just standing there, your hands clasped in front of you. And I asked why you weren't sitting down.

"I meant it as a way of telling you to go ahead and sit. But you took it as a literal question. You told me I didn't invite you to sit down. So I said I didn't need to. That you could just come in and sit. Do you remember what you told me? You said it was rude and presumptive to go into somebody's private space and sit down without a chair being offered or asking first. You never know when someone has already assigned their seats or their time. When you do that, you are assuming you're welcome and that the chair, and the time, is openly available to you."

I pull myself up a little straighter and pull my eyebrows together, deepening my voice to mimic Greg. "Just because a chair is empty doesn't mean it's available. A person who wishes to speak with you for only a moment will have you stand, a person with more time will ask you to sit. Never take a seat from someone only offering space to stand."

Eric's voice overlaps with mine for the last few words. I look up to see him coming into the room, carrying a stepladder. He offers me a sad smile.

"That was one of his favorites," he says. "I think a lot of the time, he wanted to just take the chairs out of his office and dole them out when he saw fit."

An orderly comes into the room, and my body tenses. I recognized him as the one I saw in the video stream. He comes to the edge of the bed, and I stare directly into his face. He looks back at me without flinching.

"You were here earlier," I say.

"Yes," he nods. "I work a twelve-hour shift today. I've been here for a few, and I'll be here for a few more."

"What's your name?"

"Martin," he says.

"He was here the day they brought Greg in, too," Eric tells me from his perch on the stepladder.

"How long have you worked here?" I ask.

"Five years," Martin says. "Almost six, I guess."

"Here it is," Eric says, climbing down from the ladder with a tiny black object in his palm.

"Can I get you anything?" Martin asks. "A drink or a snack? I hear you drove in from a long way."

"A drink would be great, thanks," I say, closing my eyes to chase away the suspicions.

"It was set in among the black marks on the ceiling tiles," Eric explains. "That's why it was almost impossible to see."

I take the camera from him and turn it over in my hand, looking at it.

"It's so tiny," I say.

"A lot of them are these days. People have cameras in the caps of their pens," he tells me.

"That inspires a sense of security," I note sarcastically.

"What do you want me to do with it?" he asks.

What I really want to do with the camera is throw it on the floor and smash it. But I don't.

"Put it back," I say, handing it back to him.

"What?" Eric asks.

"Put it back," I repeat. "Put it exactly where you found it."

Martin comes back with a tray holding a glass of icy soda, a can containing the rest, and a plate of cookies. He sets it down on the table beside Greg's bed.

"If you need anything else, let me know," he says. "Agent Martinez, do you want me to take that ladder for you?"

Eric holds it out for him, and he takes it before walking toward the door.

"Martin?" I call.

He turns around.

"Yes, Agent Griffin?"

"I need a pillow and some blankets. I'll be staying here tonight," I tell him.

"Be right back," he says.

"You don't have to do that," Eric says.

"Yes, I do," I reply, taking a sip of the drink. I haven't realized how thirsty I am until the sweet cold touches my tongue. I take a deep breath. Eric's still standing there with the camera, and I lift my eyebrows in expectation. "Go ahead. Put the camera back."

"Whoever sent that link has access to the stream from this camera. He'll be able to see you. He's already been here. He could come back."

"Let him come," I say.

"Emma..."

"Let him come."

## CHAPTER THIRTY-SEVEN

"Who is he, Emma?" Bellamy asks late that night.

It was a relief to discover I had actually packed a cohesive selection of clothes. I've already changed into pajamas. Around us, the floor of the hospital is quiet except for the soft beeping of machines. All the lights have been lowered, and a set of pillows and blankets wait for me on the sofa up against the wall beside Greg's bed. Eric went home a couple of hours ago, but Bellamy has lingered. I don't know if it's because she wants to spend time with me after we haven't seen each other in so long, or if she's afraid.

I would understand if she is. I know the risk I'm placing on myself by having the camera still in place. I could have had Eric disable it and bring it to the Bureau for evidence. But I want it there. I want every moment of this room captured, including me being there. Catch Me sent the link and is obviously close by. I saw the man who took Greg and who has been following me around come into the room and get ominously close to Greg. I don't know why he was there or what he was doing other than checking in on his handiwork. Like I said to Eric, let him come.

She turns to look at me.

"You said he's not your father," she says.

"He's not," I confirm.

"I saw the picture," she says.

"You also saw the scar. You told me you did."

"I did," she says. "But I don't understand what that means."

"Yes, you do, B. You know my father's scar. You remember me telling you about it happening. It was before we met, but I told you the story."

"There was a glass beer bottle in the yard behind your grandparents' house in Sherwood. He hit it with a lawnmower and it broke," she says.

"Yes," I nod. "And the glass cut his face next to his eye. So close if he had turned his head just the tiniest bit, it could have blinded him. It was a deep cut, and he had a bandage over it for weeks. I was used to that scar. It was just part of my father's face. But I know by the way people looked at him how obvious it was. Not grotesque or terrifying or anything, but it was definitely there. No one looking at him in the face would miss it. It's also not the kind of scar that would disappear. Not even after ten years. In that picture, you can see very clearly there is no scar beside that man's eye. You already know the information sent to me from Iowa. The certificate the midwife filled out. From the moment I saw it, I thought something was wrong."

"He's your father's brother," she says. "His twin."

"Yes. A twin I never knew existed. And I don't know where he came from now. But I do know he's capable of doing something like this. And if that's true, I highly doubt he wants to just stop by and get to know me."

"But why is he doing this?" Bellamy asks. "Why would he be completely invisible for your entire life, then suddenly show up and lurk around on the edge of your existence rather than just getting in touch with you? Even if it would seem incredibly strange to talk to you, it would be a lot less strange than everything he's been doing."

"You're not going to get an argument on that out of me. But I'm really tired of him. I'm tired of all of it," I sigh.

"Do you want me to stay here with you tonight?" she asks. "I've gotten pretty used to sleeping curled up in these chairs."

"No," I shake my head. "You deserve to go home and sleep in a real bed. I'll be fine here."

"Are you sure?" she asks.

"The floor is still on lockdown. All I'm going to do is curl up on the couch and sleep. I'll see you tomorrow."

She looks reluctant, but finally, she hugs me and walks out of the room, pulling the door closed behind her. I take a few more moments to stand next to Greg's bed, listening to the sound of the machines and his breath.

"I'm sorry," I whisper to him softly. "For all of it. For everything."

Lying down on the couch, I pull the blankets over me. I can feel the camera on me, but I force myself to ignore it and finally fall asleep.

---

I wake up to Eric and Martin both already in the room.

"Well, this is a new awkwardness I've never experienced," I mutter, sitting up and stretching my arms over my head. "Good morning, guys."

"Good morning," Martin says. "I brought breakfast for you if you're hungry."

I glance to where he's pointing and see a food tray covered with a pink plastic lid alongside a glass of juice wrapped in cling film. The plate looks exactly like something he would bring to one of the patients on the floor.

"He takes good care of us," Eric winks.

"I appreciate it," I say. I watch him move around Greg's bed, taking vitals and adjusting things. "What are you doing?"

"Just checking in on him. The nurses will come in shortly to do a more thorough check. Anything else you need?"

"Do you mind me asking a couple of questions?" I ask.

"No, go ahead," he nods.

I glance down at my pale green pajamas.

"Would you be more comfortable if I wasn't in pajamas?" I ask.

He laughs. "Dealing with people in pajamas is kind of my thing."

"Okay. Have you gotten familiar with the agents who have been sitting with Greg since he got here?" I ask.

"Yes," he says. "There's a specific list, and all of us on the floor were introduced to each of them before their first shift. The floor hasn't been on lockdown like it is now, but we were given pretty clear instructions about who was allowed in this room."

"How about the rest of the floor? Are people allowed to visit the patients in those rooms?

"Yes, but we are pretty familiar with the friends and family of those patients as well. This is a longer-term floor. We don't get a lot of turnover."

"Yesterday you said you were doing a twelve-hour shift. But now you're here again, bright and early in the morning. Does that happen a lot?" I ask.

"Sometimes," he shrugs. "We are short on staff pretty often. Especially this time of year with it being cold and flu season. People get sick; the hospital doesn't want them to come to work. People on these floors tend to be pretty vulnerable, as you can imagine. We had three go down this week with respiratory infections. When that happens, everybody has to do what they can to pick up the slack. Sometimes that means camping out on the cots in the break room for a few hours in between shifts."

"Sounds exhausting," I tell him.

"It definitely can be," he acknowledges. "But I don't mind. At least I don't have the pressure like the doctors do."

"There was a man in this room yesterday. He came in just shortly after you left. Do you have any idea who it was?"

"No," he shakes his head. "I did think it was odd the agents weren't here, but we aren't privy to everything. There must have been some reason they weren't needed here. Bellamy just asked me to check in on him before she left, so I assumed she knew what was going to happen."

"No, she didn't. The two agents assigned to yesterday told us they received a call from the hospital, releasing them from duty. Do you have any idea who would do that?" I ask.

He shakes his head slowly. "I don't make patient calls. The head nurse would handle everything like that. Yesterday morning it was Laura. She might be able to tell you what happened. Anything else?"

"Are there security cameras in the hallways?"

"Not on this floor. Some of the patients and events we deal with here are too sensitive to risk footage," he tells me.

"That's what I thought." I let out a sigh. "Thank you. I appreciate your help."

"I'll be back around later if you think of anything else."

He leaves, and I go over to the table, peeling away the cling film so I can take a sip of juice.

"Be right back," I tell Eric and grab my bag, bringing it with me into the bathroom.

Ten minutes later, I emerge dressed, my hair brushed, and with enough makeup to make me feel presentable. I'm still only wearing hospital-issue gripper socks, but the rest is a victory. Eric looks troubled as he stares at the tablet in his hand, rapidly flipping through screens. I sit down on the couch and pull my shoes toward me.

"What's wrong?" I ask, peeling away one gripper sock to replace it with a regular one.

"Remember the cold cases you asked me to look for?" he asks, not looking up from the screen.

I nod and stuff my foot into my boot, then repeat the process on the other side.

"Yes. The man in the cabin. I actually brought the necklace if it would help to see it," I tell him, but he's already shaking his head.

"I don't think I need to," he says.

"Did you find something?" I ask, standing up and walking over to him.

"There weren't many cases that fit all the specifications you gave. Only a few. But I think you need to see this one."

He turns the tablet toward me. For a second, I think I'm looking at Greg. Then I realize the plastic-wrapped man's body is lying on the cracked pavement of a parking lot. Bits of blond hair is visible at the top of the plastic, and I can see what looks like pictures, documents, and money rolled up with him and scattered around him.

I flip to the next screen, a scan of the autopsy report. The nondescript human form sketched on the page has arrows and slash marks to indicate all the injuries sustained on the body. One points to the neck.

"The back of his neck was bruised," I say.

"But not the front," Eric points out. "Like someone was trying to choke him backwards."

"Or tore a necklace off him."

## CHAPTER THIRTY-EIGHT

I'm still poring over the case file two hours later when Eric tells me he has to go into headquarters for I bit but would be back.

"Agent Jones is supposed to be here in about twenty minutes," he tells me.

I shake my head. "Tell him he doesn't have to come."

"Are you sure?" he asks.

"I don't need him," I say. "I'm here, and I'm not planning on going anywhere for a couple of days. Everything is essentially at a standstill with the investigation in Castleville. They're still waiting for some test results and surveillance footage from the train station, but there isn't anything else to do until they get that information. Nicolas knows if he needs me for what's going on in Feathered Nest, he can call me. Other than that, I'm not doing anything."

"Yes," Eric says sarcastically. "It sounds like your schedule is so free and clear."

"It's how I like it," I offer. "We already learned I don't relax well."

"Don't I know it," he chuckles. "Well, I shouldn't be too long. I'll get in touch with Agent Jones and tell him he doesn't need to come if you're okay being here by yourself."

"Not by myself," I tell him. "I've got Greg here."

He walks up to the couch, and I put the tablet down to stand and hug him. The amount of time we've been apart suddenly feels more real in that hug. I give him an extra squeeze just for good measure.

"It's not the best of circumstances, but it's good to have you back. Even if just temporarily," he says.

"Thank you," I say. He starts towards the door as I sit back down. "Oh, Eric. Will you see if you can find Martin and ask him to bring me some coffee? Or show me where I can get myself coffee?"

He laughs and nods. "I'm on it. Be back soon."

"See you then," I tell him.

I delve back into the cold case. As I'm reading over the autopsy report again, Martin comes into the room with a mug of coffee and a handful of creamer pods and sugar.

"I went ahead and brought you a cup. If you ever want some and I'm not around, there's a break room at the very end of the hallway on the opposite side of the floor. There's coffee and some snacks. Sometimes volunteers deliver sandwiches and stuff," he tells me.

"Thank you, Martin," I say. "You could have just told me to go to the break room and get it myself."

"It's not a problem," he says.

I empty a pod of creamer and a couple of packets of sugar into the coffee and stir it up. Usually, hospital coffee isn't the best quality, so I augment it as much as I can just so I can tolerate it. One sip tells me I've missed the mark. The drink is now so cloyingly sweet; I can't get it down. I feel bad for wasting the cup Martin brought me, but there's no way I can drink it. Setting it aside, I go back to my reading.

Just a few minutes later, the door opens. I'm not expecting anyone, so my eyes snap up to the door. They narrow slightly when I see Agent Jones coming into the room.

"Jones? What are you doing here?" I frown.

"Hey, Griffin. I heard you were back in town. On Greg duty today."

"Didn't Eric call you?" I ask. "He was just here; he was going to let you know we don't need you to come in."

"Oh," he says. "No, I didn't get that call. My service around here isn't the best, though. I might have already been in the parking deck when he tried to call me. I've been sitting down there for the last twenty-five minutes or so."

"Why?" I ask.

"I was searching my car for something. Found it in the abyss under the back passenger's seat," he tells me. "Well, I guess if you don't need me, I'll head out."

"Actually, do you mind waiting for a second?"

"Um, sure?" he raises an eyebrow, sounding confused.

"I just want to run over to the break room and grab some coffee, but I don't want to leave him alone," I explain.

Jones points at the cup beside me.

"You mean, coffee like that?" he asks.

"Oh, no. I ruined that. Just give me a second, I'll be right back."

"Okay. Greg and I will catch up on the most recent basketball scores. He has a really impressive fantasy league going on this season," he tells me.

"I'm sure he does," I say.

I leave the room with a slight smile on my face. It's good to hear everybody talk to Greg like he's there. Even if they're joking, it feels better than everybody standing around being morbid and too serious. Greg may be one of the most serious people I've ever known, but letting it weigh too heavily on us isn't going to help him. I don't know how much stock I put into the idea of healing energy, but I figure some levity and positivity couldn't make him worse, so we might as well give it a try.

An empty breakroom means I get free rein of the coffee machine. Part of a pot is already sitting there, but it seems old, so I pour it down the nearby sink and start brewing a new one. When it's done, I find a new cup, add the cream and sugar, and carry it back to the room along with a turkey sandwich wrapped in white butcher paper.

When I get back to Greg's room, Jones is actually sitting beside him, reading out basketball scores, and making comments about it. I smile.

"How's he doing?" I ask.

"Kicking everybody's ass as usual," he says. "Did you get everything you need?"

"Yep," I say, holding up my coffee and sandwich. "Thanks."

"And you're sure you don't need me?" he asks.

"I'll be fine. I have a lot to keep me occupied," I say.

"Great. Well, it was good to see you. Stop by the headquarters before you head out of town again," he tells me.

"I'll try," I say.

He leaves as I take a sip of the vastly improved coffee. My phone rings, and I set it on the arm of the couch so I can put my tablet in my lap.

"Hey," I answer when I see Dean's name on the screen. "I was actually going to call you. You would not believe what Eric found."

"I don't think you're going to believe what I found," Dean replies.

I must not have gotten enough sleep last night because my eyes suddenly feel heavy. Maybe I've been staring at the screen for too long. I shake my head and open my eyes wide to perk myself back up.

"I'm sorry, what did you say?" I ask.

"I said I don't think you're going to believe what I found," he repeats. "But you tell me first."

"Eric researched all the cold cases that matched the man from the cabin. We think we found him."

"Seriously?" Dean asks.

"Yeah. Perfectly matches the description, and he was wrapped in plastic, just like Greg. The autopsy report even mentions a deep bruise on the back of his neck. Like a necklace was yanked off."

"Where did they find him?"

"In Florida. He was dumped in the parking lot of an old hotel that had been torn down and was under construction. There was no identification on the body. No driver's license or passport. The only thing they found was a label on the inside of his jacket collar. It said Murdock."

"That's incredible," Dean says.

It sounds like his voice is coming at me from a far distance. My head swims, and I fight to keep my eyes open. My heart feels like it's trembling slightly in my chest. I try to ignore it. I'm just exhausted, and I'm probably dealing with the adrenaline dump after the race to get here yesterday. Dean is saying something, but I don't understand any of it.

"What was that?" I ask. "I missed it."

"Are you doing alright, Emma?" he asks.

"I'm fine," I sigh. "Just really tired. Tell me what you found."

"I went to the hospital," he tells me.

"Did you get inside?" I ask.

"I did. Turns out there were a lot of former patients of the Rolling View Hospital who didn't make the move over to the new facility," he says.

"You found the records room," I say, feeling slightly more breathless.

"Not only did I find the record room, I found your mother's file. We've officially made it through the looking-glass. I found our Alice."

Black spots are dancing in front of my eyes and my skin tingles. I try to speak, to tell Dean what's going on, but suddenly it's like my lips won't work. I only hear him say one more sentence before everything goes black.

"Your mother's nurse was Alice Logan."

# CHAPTER THIRTY-NINE

One night when I was a little girl, an earthquake hit our area. It came in the middle of the night, so I was in bed. It woke me up, but I wasn't aware of what was going on around me. I thought someone was standing beside the bed, shaking the mattress. Maybe my father was being silly and jumping on the bed again. He'd done it before when I wouldn't get out of bed in time to go to school. But it was still dark. It wasn't time to go to school yet.

It took a few seconds for me to get my eyes all the way open and my brain clear enough to realize there was nobody by the bed. But everything was shaking. I was so scared I couldn't move. I just lied there on my bed, hanging onto my sheets and wondering if the ceiling fan was secure enough so it wouldn't fall and hurt me.

It probably only lasted a few seconds, but it felt like an eternity. When the shaking finally stopped, it still felt like my body was trembling. For a long time, I wondered if aftershocks of an earthquake could be so isolated, so only I would have been able to feel them. That was the only earthquake I ever felt, but I never forgot it.

The memory immediately comes to mind as my consciousness starts to come back. I can't open my eyes. I can feel my body but can't move. The ground below me is shaking, and I want to hold on to something beside me, but I can't get my hands to cooperate. A few seconds later, everything goes black again. I don't know how long I'm out, but it's probably not long. When I wake up again, I'm still moving, and I become aware of layers of sound. The rhythmic rumble beneath me is like wheels. Voices speak in hushed tones to each other. Somewhere in the background, there's the soft beeping of machines.

I'm still in the hospital. But why can't I wake up? There's something over my face. It's not stopping me from breathing, but the sensation of it touching my nose and mouth makes my lungs constrict. As I keep moving, I realize I'm on a stretcher. I try to make a noise to get the attention of anyone around me but can't force my voice out of my throat. Moments later, I'm asleep again.

This time when I open my eyes, my skin stings with cold. I'm not moving anymore. Everything is still around me, and I can no longer hear any of the sounds. Consciousness rolls through me, bringing me more and more out of the sleep with every breath I manage to take. The sheet is no longer over my face, but when I open my eyes, I see only darkness.

I manage to move my hand slightly to the side and feel cold metal. Panic starts to build, worsening as the blackness creeps in around the edges of my eyes again. I can feel myself being dragged back down into the sleep, but I try to fight it. I try to stay awake, to pull myself into a sharper state of mind. But it's no use. My eyes close and again I'm lost.

By the time I wake up again, the cold is so deep in my bones, it hurts. I'm struggling to breathe in, and my fingers tingle and sting. I force myself to move them, to reach out to either side of me. Again, I only feel cold metal. The smell around me burns my throat and turns my stomach. I know where I am. There are few places in the world that can mimic the drawer in a morgue.

Gathering every bit of my energy and strength, I kick at the end of the drawer. It makes a hollow clanging sound and sends a shock of new pain rattling up my leg. But I don't care. I have to try again.

This time I reach deep into my chest and find my voice. Battling to push away the feeling of sleep wanting to take over again, I kick hard and let out what I hope is a scream. It's nowhere near as loud as I want it to be. I muster more to try again. With every kick and every scream, I struggle and fight to force the exhaustion away. It's barely enough. But I can't give up. I have to keep fighting.

I struggle and scream and thrash around with every ounce of strength. It's working. Slowly, but it's working. Soon I'm loud enough anybody walking past can hear. But I can't sustain it for long.

The cold is affecting every part of my body, and panic is starting to settle in over the adrenaline, making it harder to breathe. I don't know how long I've been in here or how I got here. All I know is I need to get out fast.

I scream out again, but my voice is getting weaker. I'm losing air too quickly.

Suddenly I hear a click in the distance that sounds like a door opening. Relief finally washes over me. I kick again. The drawer jostles, and suddenly I'm being yanked forward. I'm about to thank whoever rescued me when his face appears, hovering over mine. Somewhere in the distance, I'm aware of the sound of an alarm as eyes that look like mine stare at me and a mouth that looks like my father's curves into a smile.

"Hi, Emma," my uncle says.

I draw in a deep breath and try to move, but I'm not fast enough. His hands grab me by the front of my shirt, and he pulls me up off the cold slab.

"Stop," I groan.

"Emma," he says. "Emma, look at me."

His voice had sounded muffled, but now it's clear and familiar. I force my eyes open to look at him. It's no longer my uncle's face staring at me. Instead, it's Dean Steele.

I sag in his arms, and he scoops me up against his chest. He runs out into the hallway, and the sound of the alarm becomes piercing.

"I have her," he calls out to someone. "She's right here."

A few moments later, I'm out of his arms and on another bed, but this one is warm and soft. It starts to move, and I panic, my hands clamping down on either side of me. A hand smooths down over my hair.

"You're alright," Dean whispers. "You're alright now. We're going to get you to a room. Just hang on."

The next hour is a blur as I try to regain my grasp on consciousness and reality. Doctors and nurses swarm in and out, and two uniformed police officers come to the side of my bed to pepper me with questions.

"What happened?"

"Who did this to you?"

"Were you injected with something?"

"What did you eat?"

"What did you drink?"

I have no answers for them. I tell them everything I remember, from waking up on the couch that morning to waking up in the morgue. Suddenly a thought snaps into my head.

"Greg," I say. "Has anybody checked on Greg?"

"He's fine," Dean says. "Eric and Bellamy are there. I'm going to go let them know you're alright while the doctors check you over more thoroughly."

―――

With the exception of the chill from the morgue and the disorienting effect of whatever sedative I was given, I'm fine. I learn I was missing for at least two hours, and they only realized it when a nurse heard my phone ringing in Greg's room and answered it to hear Dean upset because I'd stopped talking to him so suddenly. He'd left Feathered Nest early that morning to come into town with the medical records he unearthed. He knew I was busy and likely wouldn't be going back for at least a few days, but he didn't want to wait to show me what he found.

Thank goodness he didn't. If it wasn't for him demanding they contact Eric or Bellamy, no one would have realized I was missing, and I'd still be in the morgue drawer. Or with whoever stuffed me there. I can only think of two options. And that's far too many.

Eric and Bellamy rush into the room and come to my bedside. I brush away their fussing, done with being emotional. At least I'm going to pretend for their sake. In reality, I am scared shitless. It takes some time to convince the doctors I don't need to be admitted and to finish my report with the police. When both are done, I'm finally allowed to go back to Greg's room and curl up on the couch. I won't be staying here tonight, but I'll stay for a while longer.

Suddenly, Sam bursts into the room, his eyes wild.

"Emma," he gasps, running to the side of the couch and dropping down to a crouch so he can wrap his arms around me. "What the hell happened?"

"I don't know," I tell him. I go over the story with him, and he pulls me against him again, kissing me.

"I love you," he whispers.

"I love you, too."

"How does something like this happen?" he demands, standing up and stalking through the room as if he's just trying to find someone to blame. He turns back to me. "Emma, I need you to listen to me. I know you've been insisting that this Catch Me guy and your uncle are not the same person."

"They aren't," I cut him off. "They aren't the same person. And if you think there's only one person, you're only going to look for one person. There are two."

"The postcard you got with the link that showed the video of Greg's room. That was from Catch Me," he says.

"Yes," I say.

"But it showed your father's brother come into Greg's room. Don't you think it's a little convenient if it's two people, one would just know the other had planted a camera?" he asks.

"Yes, that would be very convenient. But not the other way around," I say.

"What?" he asks.

"You keep insisting that my father's brother is Catch Me. But it doesn't make sense. One is following me; the other is tormenting me. It's very unlikely my uncle would know the camera was planted in the room and show up just to scare me. But it's very likely Catch Me knew he was going to the hospital and put the camera there so I could see him there. Catch Me isn't my father's brother, Sam. But he definitely knows who he is and what he's doing. They're orbiting each other, and it's just a matter of time before they crash."

"Emma," Bellamy's voice says from behind Sam.

She left soon after I got back to this room to see if she could get better luck getting Greg's chart, but now she's standing at the door with fear in her eyes.

"Bells, what's wrong?" I ask.

She draws in a breath.

"A supply closet was raided, and there are several scalpels missing. One of the rooms had all the linens stripped from the bed, and they're unaccounted for. But it's not just that."

"What else?"

"Martin's gone."

**THE END**

Six books down and one more to go!

Book 7 will be the grand finale for this season of Emma Griffin adventures. Be sure to check it out as it will answer all the questions you may have so far!

I hope you enjoyed this sixth book in the Emma Griffin series. I appreciate your continued support! No worries if this is the first book you read, all the paperbacks are available at Amazon.com and most online retailers.

If you enjoyed this book, please leave me a review on Amazon! Your

reviews allow me to get the validation to keep this series going and also helps attract new readers.
Just a moment of your time is all that is needed.

I promise to always do my best to bring you thrilling adventures.

Yours,
A.J. Rivers

P.S. If for some reason you didn't like this book or found typos or other errors, please let me know personally. I do my best to read and respond to every email at aj@riversthrillers.com

# MORE EMMA GRIFFIN FBI MYSTERIES

*Emma Griffin's FBI Mysteries* is the new addictive best-selling series by A.J. Rivers. Make sure to get them all below!

Visit my author page on Amazon to order your missing copies now! Now available in paperback!

## STAYING IN TOUCH WITH A.J.

Type the link below in your internet browser now to join my mailing list and get your free copy of Edge Of The Woods.

## STAYING IN TOUCH WITH A.J.

https://dl.bookfunnel.com/ze03jzd3e4

ALSO BY A.J. RIVERS

The Girl and the Hunt
The Girl and the Deadly Express
The Girl Next Door
The Girl in the Manor
The Girl That Vanished
The Girl in Cabin 13
Gone Woman

Printed by Amazon Italia Logistica S.r.l.
Torrazza Piemonte (TO), Italy